Synopsis

Down on his luck from a few untimely investments, retired Colonial Forces Captain Jonathan Vandoc accepts a risky offer to pilot a freighter to Kublai; the only neutral port with access to the outer Perseus Arm of our galaxy, an area under control of the Khan. Captain Vandoc's misfortune is only compounded when he is abducted by the Khan's forces and sentenced to a lifetime of hard labor in an undisclosed penal colony, on a forbidden volcanic moon, deep within the Kingdom.

Vandoc's action-packed escape is a captivating tale of mystery, self-transcendence, survival, wits, and poetic justice as he not only discovers a clever way off the moon, but that his escape may have been prophesied in the ancient religious texts of the Pawani; settlers who arrived in the area long before the Khan.

The
Legendary Escape
of Captain Vandoc

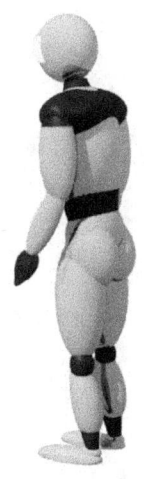

Donald Hanzel

Cubikos Orbital Command Center: 4479 A.D.

"Look at this," Private Norlo says, staring at a blinking dot on a floating screen.

"What is it, private?" Lt Farland asks.

"I don't know, sir" Norlo answers. "It's blinking. It may be a distress signal."

"What's its point of origin?" Farland asks.

"The middle of nowhere," Norlo replies. "I think it's an amplified beacon transmission of some kind, coming from some uncharted point in the Perseus-Sagittarius gap, beneath the galactic plane."

"Damn," Lt. Farland replies as he stares over Norlo's shoulder at the screen.

"What would someone be doing way out in the Great Divide?" Private Norlo asks.

"Your guess is as good as mine," Farland answers; "but if it is a distress signal and these readouts are accurate, we're twelve-hundred years too late to help. That's a slow-band signal, sent from the Colonial Era."

Chapter 1

Twelve hundred twenty-four years earlier: Christmas Eve 3255 A.D.

"Between you and me," Nario tells Vandoc as he watches a star streak by the bridge porthole; "Kublai has more culture than anywhere else in the galaxy. I think you'll enjoy your visit."

"What is it that you like so much about it?" Vandoc asks.

"Two radically different worlds converge at one point," Nario answers; "the most contentious point in the galaxy," he adds with a smile. "That fosters a unique culture."

"Uniquely dangerous," Vandoc replies.

"Yes," Nario responds; "but that adds that extra excitement to the journey. I'm surprised you haven't been here before. Didn't you captain for the Colonies during the war?" he asks.

"I did," Vandoc answers; "but the conflict had wound down by the time I enlisted. I spent most of the war flying commercial freight."

"So, you've never been this far out?" Nario asks.

"I can't say that I have," Vandoc replies cunningly, knowing the reply to be literally valid.

"Prepare for ringway deceleration and arrival at New Kublai's South Port," a soft female voice announces following a pong.

"Here we are, Captain, at the edge of the civilized galaxy. We're a long way from home," Nario says as he gently backhands Vandoc's shoulder.

"Indeed, we are," Vandoc replies with a less comfortable look on his face.

"It's still Christmas Eve you know, which is recognized in South Kublai. Let's check in, then grab a bite," Nario says. "The food in Kublai is worth the trip alone, and I know a great place."

"Sounds good," Vandoc replies. "I just need to check in with Neb before she reports me missing," he adds.

"Oh yes," Nario responds, nodding with a look of familiarity before looking away to avoid Vandoc's gaze.

"You and Nebula were close back in the day," Vandoc notes, reading Nario's face. "Were you two ever a thing?" Vandoc asks.

"I thought you knew," Nario answers. "It was a really long time ago. I'm sure it just wasn't worth mentioning."

"No, she never mentioned it," Vandoc replies with a surprised but cool-with-it look on his face.

"It was nothing, believe me," Nario replies; "short lived."

The first ring of the ringway appears in front of them in perfect alignment. Within seconds, the ship flies bulls-eye through the center of it, then another and another, slowing significantly between each ring. Kublai appears brightly in the ship's forepane as their DeepShore freighter emerges from the final ring. Vandoc and Nario both sit in awe as the craft glides closer to the brilliant planet.

"Entering Kublai's atmosphere," the voice announces. "Prepare to dock in nineteen minutes, thirty-seven seconds, mark."

Fire envelops their vessel as it sinks into Kublai's atmosphere. The fire is brief, however, as Kublai's *Glass Sea* comes into view beneath an endless pastel purple sky. Their spacecraft swoons before leveling into a holding pattern above the water's breathing blue surface.

"Oh, the things rumored to live within those waters," Vandoc tells Nario.

"Not a good place to go down," Nario says.

"No, let us stay aloft," Vandoc replies with a laugh.

"Don't forget to exit the ship port side after we dock in the Neutral Zone," Nario reminds Vandoc. "We don't want to end up inadvertently in North Kublai."

Alas, the *Glass Sea* cliffs come into view, as does the City of Kublai. The ship glides over the heart of the city and into the massive Neutral Zone, then slows before coming to a stop and docking at Berth 33. Vandoc and Nario grab their bags and wait for clearance at the flight deck's port side door lock. A red light on the door changes to green. Nario pulls a lever within the craft and the door opens. The men step onto an enormous platform. The door closes behind them, after which the starboard side doors open, allowing the North Kublai crew to board the craft and begin unloading its payload.

Vandoc and Nario grab a train to their hotel; The Seasons. Once there, they check in and agree to meet again in the lobby an hour later for dinner. In his room, Vandoc plugs into the house fon to check for any messages from Nebula. He has two:

- "Hi Van, just thinking about you," the first one says. "Hope you arrive safely."
- "Just thinking about you. Let me know when you arrive," her second one says.

Vandoc transmits a message back to her:

"I've arrived safely in Kublai," he tells her. "I miss you, babe and wish we could be together. It's Christmas Eve," he adds with a sad sigh in his voice. "Anyway, I'll be back just in time for New Year's, but I'm not looking forward to another forty-nine hours on that ship," he says with a pause. "I'm getting along well with Nario," he adds. "We've gotten to know each other better." Vandoc pauses again, then looks at the camera. "I'll see you soon." He signs off.

Chapter 2

The Glass Sea fades into infinity from the lobby's bay windows. Vandoc stares at it. The water is so still, cross-fading between reflections of Kublai's southern green aurora and a shimmering deep purple glow of the Rosette Nebula, prominent on dark Kublai nights.

Nario soon arrives and the two men step out into New Kublai's lively entertainment district. Nario guides Vandoc through a confounding maze of small cobblestone streets filled with bustling markets. Within minutes they arrive at *Microns*, a charming restaurant and martini bar tucked into an ancient side street that runs along the edge of the city's dividing wall. They are immediately seated at a table.

"The stark contrast between life here and what lies just a few feet north of us, is hard to imagine," Vandoc tells Nario.

"I appreciate you helping me out," Nario tells Vandoc. "My regular pilot had some family issues and I was in a pinch. I know this is not the most desirable route in the galaxy."

"It interests me. I've read a lot about the ancient history behind this city, the Khan and his ancient Mongol creeds used to rule the Kingdom," Vandoc tells him, now wishing he could mention more about his previous missions here.

"Is that why you took this run?" Nario asks.

"Partially," Vandoc answers, now looking over a menu.

"What else would drive you sixty-one thousand light years from home on Christmas?" Nario inquires.

"I need the additional revenue." Vandoc answers.

"You must be doing pretty well," Nario says. "You've got a canyon-rim condo on Mars."

"Its property value is sinking as terraforming issues have sparked fear throughout the whole Martian housing market," Vandoc replies. "We got in at the peak and seem to be stuck holding a dropping ball."

"Ouch," Nario replies.

"Yeah, Nebula was the one who wanted a place on Mars," Vandoc says. "Now she seems to hate everything about it, and it's as if I'm to blame. Even the faint, distant sound of the Canyon Express bothers her. You can barely hear that train at night, so far off in the distance, but that's where she is; so far away."

"Sorry to hear it," Nario responds.

"It's even worse," Vandoc replies; "to make up for it, I invested heavily into Iridium in the Martian futures market. This was just before the Khan's supply was approved for the Colonies and Iridium contracts plummeted. They're still in freefall."

"Martian futures are known to be volatile; the highest risk investments in the solar system," Nario replies.

"With market proximity laws, I had no other investment options," Vandoc tells him; "as a Martian resident that is."

"I see," Nario responds. "I might be able to get you more flights if you need the work."

"Thanks, I may," Vandoc responds just as a blue light illuminates on his fon. "I never really wanted it, you know."

"What?" Nario asks.

"The condo, the whole lifestyle…" Vandoc answers.

"Excuse me, Vandoc," Nario interjects with a smile as he sees a familiar face at the bar. The face smiles back. It's a tall, thin man with long, blond hair, dapperly dressed. He approaches the table. Nario invites him to sit.

"Vandoc, this is Maxiums Krylok, a real live North Kublain," Nario says. "He works for the Khan."

"Nario has spoken highly of your skills, Captain," Maxiums tells Vandoc.

"Thank you," Vandoc says, not expecting to meet a member of the Khanate. The two men exchange quick bows. "So, what brings you to South Kublai?" Vandoc asks.

"Diplomatic immunity," Nario jumps in to answer. "Maxiums is free to travel between Kublai and New Kublai."

"Yes, but only within New Kublai," Maxiums answers; "not throughout the Colonies."

"Who do you work for?" Vandoc asks.

"The Khan," Maxiums answers. "Ministry of Trade," he adds after a brief pause. "If there is anything I can do for you, please let me know."

Vandoc's fon lights up. "Please excuse me. I have to use a com-box. Is there one around here?" he asks Nario.

"Yes, use the one just outside this restaurant," Nario answers. "Remember to take the spiral stairwell just out the door and to the left. There's a com-box at the base of the stairs."

"Got it," Vandoc says.

Once outside, Vandoc finds the stairwell and descends into a dim alley. A light guides him to a com-box. He enters and closes the door behind him. Inside, he plugs into the central fon. As hoped, he has a new message from Nebula.

- "Hi Van," she begins. "I know it's physically impossible to hear from you yet, so far away. I just hope you've arrived safely by the time you get this message. I miss you."

Vandoc smiles, comforted to hear Neb's voice.

"I miss you too," he replies. "I'm having dinner with Nario. I'll send another message after I get back to my room." He hits send.

As he steps out of the com-box, however, he realizes he is not in the same alley. He is completely turned around. How could this be? There is no spiral staircase, nor any staircase for that matter. He can see only a fraction of the street above but no way to get there. Confused, he backtracks into the alley, then turns a different corner to look for the stairwell. There is no stairwell. Nothing is familiar.

The street descends into a dark tunnel. With high stone walls on each side, there appears to be only one available way to go; through it. Once through, it leads around another dark corner.

Beside a cascading flow of drainage water, Vandoc spots a woman in a long black robe. She is standing with her back to him. He approaches her.

"Excuse me, I somehow got turned around coming out of the com-box. How do I get back to Microns?" he asks. The woman turns and smiles. She is elderly.

"Microns, did you say?" she asks with a soft weak voice.

"Yes," the captain answers with a smile.

The woman smiles again, then gently takes him by the arm.

"Come," she says; "you need to take the spiral stairwell."

"Yes," Vandoc softly shouts, relieved. "Thank you!"

The woman slowly guides the captain around a dark corner and into a dark, dead-ended alley.

"Wait here," she tells him. "They will take you to the spiral staircase."

"Who?" Vandoc asks.

"Just wait," the old woman says. "They know the way."

Moments later, two men appear in matching, unmarked uniforms of some kind. They approach Vandoc and the woman.

"He's looking for Microns," the woman tells the uniformed men.

"We got it," the taller of the two replies while digitally transferring some kind of credit into the woman's bracelet. The woman thanks him, then walks away.

"Can you take me to the spiral stairwell?" Vandoc asks the men.

"Sir, we are law enforcement," one of the men says. "We can help you. Can we see some identification?" he asks.

"Sure," Vandoc answers, handing over his Colonial Passport ID chip. "Why did you pay that lady?" he asks.

"It's just customary here," the officer replies while scanning his chip. A readout appears. Both uniformed men look at each other confidently. One speaks.

"Captain Vandoc," he says; "you are aware that you are in the City of North Kublai, are you not?" he asks.

The captain's heart sinks to his knees.

"How can that be?" Vandoc desperately asks. "That simply can't be."

"So, you are saying that you are unintentionally in the Kingdom of Khan?" the other of the two interrogating officers asks.

"Something happened in that com-box," Vandoc says with confusion in his voice. "It must have spun around, or slowly descended, or something while I was using it. Who's doing this? Who are you guys?"

"Relax Captain," the taller officer tells him. "We'll sort this out.

The uniformed men continue to examine Vandoc's identification as he grows impatient. Finally, they speak to him.

"You lack documentation. Please come with us so we can get to the bottom of this," the taller of the two requests.

"I'm having dinner with a travel companion," Vandoc tells them. "I need to get back to Microns."

"We'll work this out as soon as we can," the shorter officer tells him. "The sooner you come, the sooner we can resolve this."

The uniformed men walk Vandoc several blocks away, to an unmarked building. Once inside, they ask him to wait alone in a small white room furnished with only a small table and two chairs. Vandoc, exhausted, complies. He takes a seat. Within minutes, he starts to lose his mind, however. He gets up and tries the door, but it is locked. He pounds on it and yells, "I want a lawyer!"

Nearly an hour later, the door opens and in walks a man dressed in what looks to be Khanate formal wear. He stares at Vandoc, then motions the two guards who came with him to wait outside. He takes a seat at the table, across from Vandoc.

"Captain Vandoc," the man says. "My name is Poray and I'm with Khanate Intelligence. I am your attorney."

"Attorney?" Vandoc asks in shock. "What have I done? Why have I been put in this room?"

"Captain, you are being charged by the Khanate with espionage," Poray replies.

"Espionage!" Vandoc shouts. "I am a Shorebok Shipping freighter pilot that somehow ended up in North Kublai. This is all some kind of huge mistake."

"Yes," Poray calmly responds; "about that, did you use to pilot for a company called Corridor Freight?"

"Decades ago," Vandoc answers. "Why?"

"During the war?" Poray asks.

"Before the war," Vandoc replies; "and maybe until shortly after it broke out."

"That's what they're interested in," Poray tells him with a look of fear on his face.

"Wait," Vandoc says; "who are *they*?" he asks. "You're with Khanate Intelligence."

"Captain, you are being put before a military tribunal in the morning. Your case is not considered a civil or criminal case but moreover an act of war."

"Okay," Vandoc says. "I've complied. I've done everything I was asked to do. I have not been defiant. This, however, is BAT-SHIT crazy! I leave a restaurant to make a call, walk out of the wrong exit, and now I'm somehow a SPY! For fuck's sake, get me the hell out of here!"

"Captain, is there anything you can tell me to bolster your case?"

"What could I possibly tell you? None of this makes any sense. Can I make a fon call?"

"You can, but not beyond the Kingdom," Poray answers.

"So, I can't even contact anyone in South Kublai?" Vandoc questions. "You are the only person I know here. Just what am I supposed to do?"

"I'll be really honest here," Poray tells him. "Things don't look good for you. Do you know anyone at all in the Kingdom?" he asks.

"Like who?" Vandoc asks.

"Anyone," Poray responds; "in Kublai, you're dealing with corruption. Money and power are what these people respond to best."

"Wait," Vandoc tells him. "I just met a diplomat from the Khanate who offered to help me."

"Who?' Poray asks.

"Maxiums Krylok," Vandoc answers.

"Maxiums Krylok?" Poray asks with a look of confusion on his face.

"Yes," Vandoc answers. "Do you know who he is?"

"No," Poray replies, "but I'll look into it right away. What position does he hold?"

"I don't know," Vandoc answers, "but he works with the Ministry of Trade. I was just with him at Microns in South Kublai when I got forced into the street and found myself in North Kublai."

"Let me check into this for you," Poray tells him. "Time is of the essence."

"Please do. And thank you," Vandoc replies. "Anything you can do for me, I'll repay you. I promise."

Poray signals to the guards through a small window on the door. When they open the door, he leads Vandoc to a holding cell; just an empty room with a padded bench.

"You can rest here and I'll be back before morning," Poray says.

"Find Maxiums Krylok," Vandoc replies. "Please, I've got a wife waiting for me at home."

"I'll do everything I can," Poray tells him as he leaves the room.

Captain Vandoc pulls his fon out of his pocket. Odd that they haven't taken it. He checks its track mapping and can retrace his course to the com-box. From there it goes black. It shows no mode of connection. He puts it away, sits back and sighs. None of this makes any sense.

Every fiber in Vandoc's body wants him to scream, to fight, to run, but he keeps his cool. His constraint is fueled by a deeply seeded fear. He understands the Kingdom, the Khan, and the Khanate far greater than your average Colonist does. Along with astronautical engineering, it was an obsession of his. Vandoc knows too well that he's in deepening trouble.

To have served against the Khan in the war is construed throughout the Kingdom to be a crime and carries a mandatory death sentence. Lie detection devices of this time are precise, even within the Kingdom. Were Vandoc to be asked under sanctioned lie detection if he'd served in the war against the Khan, he would have to answer "yes." Fortunately, they are rarely used in the Kingdom, largely due to the level of lying found throughout the governing Khanate. Liars naturally hate truth machines.

Exhausted, Vandoc lies on the padded bench, staring up at the lights on the ceiling. He takes a deep breath and finds himself at peace, as if he's already accepted his fate. Maybe I'm here because I deserve to be, he thinks. The military had warned time and again to avoid Kublai, that more was at stake for him than other travelers. What will Nebula think? He wonders. Will she ever even know? Though every cell in his body cries for rest, his racing mind rejects their screams. He is puzzled and knows that he has to figure this one out.

Sunlight eventually cracks the room, light from the massive star Genghis. Vandoc hasn't slept. He knows how draconian Khanate laws can be. He's also heard the rumors and read the news of some colonials who've simply disappeared from Kublai in the past. Could this be what's happening to him? Recent years have been quiet, but his suspicions continue to grow with every passing minute. Where is Poray? Has he found Maxiums Krylok?

Poray finally returns. The look on his face, however, is not encouraging. He sits on the bench next to Vandoc.

"They're here," he tells Vandoc. "We have to go to trial now."

"Here?" Vandoc asks. "What about Maxiums Krylok? Were you able to find him?"

"I'm sorry," Poray answers. "There is no Ministry of Trade. I did check the House of Commerce and Trade, but there was nobody registered there by that name."

"Have you tried public registries?" Vandoc asks.

"Everything," Poray replies; "I'm sorry."

"You've got to help me," Vandoc tells Poray. "This is some kind of set-up. I've done nothing wrong at all. Can you contact my wife?"

"I'm sorry Captain," Poray tells him. "Communication is forbidden outside of the Kingdom, even for me."

"What about when it's necessary for legal research?" Vandoc asks.

"There are exceptions," Poray tells him. "Look, I could be at risk. Your case is military, meaning it is not published anywhere in public Khanate records. You're considered a risk to the Kingdom's security. I could be in deep trouble for aiding or abetting you in any way that goes beyond legal representation."

"You're all I've got," Vandoc tells him.

"I'll keep you in mind," Poray says with a nod of confidence.

Poray taps on the door and the guards let them out of the cell. They are escorted down a hall and into a small room with an elevated table at its front. Seated behind the table is an older woman with gray hair, dressed in ceremonial military wear. She looks so stern, so callous from years of blind service to the

Khan. There is a gavel on the desk in front of her. She picks it up and strikes its sound block twice.

"This court is now in order," she says without even giving Vandoc or Poray a chance to take a seat. "You may sit down," she then says. They do so. "Captain Vandoc," she says. "You are being charged with espionage. How do you plead?"

"Not guilty, ma'am," Vandoc answers.

"You will address me as 'Your Excellence' when in my court," the judge yells as she strikes the sound block once again.

"Not guilty, Your Excellence," Vandoc restates.

"Is the prosecution ready to state its case?" the judge asks.

"Yes, Your Excellence," answers one of the guys in military uniform who escorted them to the room, apparently the acting prosecutor. "Captain Vandoc was discovered in the Wall District undocumented. We don't know how or why he entered the Kingdom. Our background checks, however, lead us to his prior work for Corridor Freight, a company suspected of supplying parts to the Colonies during the war. Captain Vandoc has admitted to this."

"I've simply admitted to working for them," Vandoc interjects.

"Silence," the judge demands, pounding the gavel. "You may only speak when asked to in this court. Do you understand, Captain?"

The Legendary Escape of Captain Vandoc

"I do, Your Excellence," Vandoc answers.

"Good," the judge replies. "Now, are you saying that you did work for Corridor Freight?" she asks.

"I did work for Corridor," Vandoc answers. "If that company supplied the war effort, I had no knowledge of such activities," he adds, now knowing that he's out on a limb.

"When did you work for Corridor?" the judge asks.

"Approximately twenty-two earth years ago," Vandoc answers.

"Yes, during the war," the judge notes. "How did you enter the Kingdom?" she asks.

"Inadvertently, Your Excellence. I have no idea, I swear. I was using a com-box in South Kublai. When I walked out, I was in a different place, somewhere here in the Kingdom. I mean no harm or disrespect to you, the Khan or the Kingdom. I simply ask to be returned to my life," Vandoc pleads.

There is a minute of silence as the judge looks over the information in front of her. Vandoc stews in his deepest fears. Finally, she speaks.

"Captain Vandoc, please rise," she says. The captain stands straight and tall. "Captain, for the charge of illegal entry and trespassing, I find you guilty. For the greater charge of espionage, I also find you guilty," she says, striking the block again. "You are sentenced to a lifetime of hard labor, to be served at an undisclosed location. Have you anything to say?" she asks.

After sitting silently for a moment in sheer shock, Vandoc speaks to the few members of the court.

"Have I anything to say?" Vandoc redirects the question to the court. "What would you have to say?" he then asks. "What would you say if you were abducted, arrested, put on trial for espionage for Christ's sake in some ass-backward kangaroo court?" he yells. "What would you say? Well for starters, how about fuck you, and that punky prosecutor too. In fact, fuck the whole lot of you...," Vandoc yells as the judge again strikes her gavel.

"Take him away," she orders; "before I change my mind and give him death."

"Please," Vandoc begs Poray as guards drag him away; "find Maxiums Krylok for me. Tell him what happened."

Chapter 3

Back on Mars, a warm wind whips out of the canyon, catching Agent Sandbrook and Inspector Perry by surprise as they follow a walkway along its rim.

"Lines," Sandbrook tells Perry; "and this one was the biggest one of them all; so straight they thought they were canals," he adds, as they follow a private walk leading to a cliffside condominium. "It was all they could see at the time."

"This is it," Perry tells Sandbrook as they approach the door and ring the bell.

A soft chime alerts Nebula to the arrival of guests. She pauses, then gets up from the comfort of her condo's canyon view terrace to answer the door. She checks the monitor to find two men standing outside her entrance; one in uniform and the other in semi-business attire. She touches the monitor to grant them entry. Once inside, the man in business attire introduces himself and his associate.

"Hello Ms. Cranston," he says. "I'm Agent Sandbrook with the Colonial Allied Forces and this is Inspector Perry with Martian Law Enforcement. "We spoke earlier."

"Yes, gentlemen," Nebula answers; "please come in." She invites them into her living room. "Would you care for anything to drink?" she asks. The men look at each other and politely signal their decline.

"We just have a few questions for you, "Agent Sandbrook tells her."

"Of course," Nebula replies. "Have you heard anything yet?"

"No, not yet," Officer Perry answers.

"Ms. Cranston, when was the last time you spoke with your husband?" Agent Sandbrook asks.

"Before he left, of course," she answers. "We couldn't speak face to face from that point on, but we did exchange messages."

"What was the last message you sent him before learning that he was missing?" Agent Sandbrook asks.

"I sent him a message on Christmas Eve, asking if he'd arrived and when he'd be returning," she said. "I received a reply, but it was the last I heard from him.

"Was it received?" the agent asks.

"The first one I sent was," she answered. "He replied. I don't know about the second one. He never replied to that one. Next thing I know, Nario sent me a message saying that he couldn't find Vandoc."

"How long have you known Nario Shorebok," Agent Sandbrook asks.

"We go back to high school," Nebula answers.

"Did the two of you ever date?" the agent asks.

"No, we're just close friends," Nebula answers, somewhat taken aback. "We did briefly have something going, but it didn't last," she adds. "I wouldn't call it dating. Why are you asking me this?" she asks. "My husband is lost. Can you find him?"

"Trust me ma'am, that's exactly what we're trying to do," Agent Sandbrook assures her. "It's protocol for us to ask these questions."

"I understand," she says.

"Have you taken any life insurance out on your husband?" the agent asks.

"No," Nebula answers. "Vandoc handles most of our finances."

"Are you aware of any policies on him?" Agent Sandbrook continues.

"No," Nebula answers. "I suppose there may be some insurance through his military service, but I don't know anything about that."

"Nothing at all?" the agent asks.

"Nothing," Nebula answers. "Agent Sandbrook, I love my husband. I would give anything I have to have him back home."

"Ms. Cranston, I want to thank you for your time," the agent tells her. "Rest-assured, we are doing everything we can to locate your husband."

"Thank you, Agent Sandbrook," Nebula replies. "I can't sleep. I'm on pins and needles. Please bring him home to me."

Chapter 4

Sixty-one thousand light years from Mars, a prison freighter enters the atmosphere of the legendary moon *Pyro* as it begins its descent to the lunar surface. The ship glides over *Mt. Dyvok*, Pyro's most famous and one of its most active volcanoes, before finally setting down within the endless walls of the undisclosed penal colony of New Pompeii.

Upon touchdown, prisoners are forced to remove all clothing and surrender everything they have in their possession. Those who refuse, or even hesitate, are shocked into submission with cattle prods. Vandoc quickly assesses the situation and realizes there's no value in resisting, at least not at this point. He strips nude and tosses his clothing and fon into a bin as he exits the craft. With a few dozen other prisoners, he steps off the vessel, stripped of everything, into an atmosphere so polluted he can taste it. The air is hot. The prisoners are made to walk barefoot onto a sulfurous stench-ridden field, across soft, mushy terrain where they are forced to form in lines in front of a stone platform. Soon, a large, long-haired man in military uniform steps onto the platform and up to a podium that rests center-stage. He stares over the men for a solid minute without saying a solitary word, relishing the fear in the prisoners' eyes. Finally, he speaks.

"I am Colonel Creed," he says before pausing again. "You are here because you have violated the laws of the Khan. You may feel you have been wrongly imprisoned. I do not care. You are guilty of something. Who you were before that ship touched down is neither here nor there," Creed yells; "and who you are now is nobody. You are no different to me than the piss roaches that infest your bunks. Your possessions will burn in Mt. Dyvok, and sooner or later, so will your bones. None of your friends nor family members knows where you are. Over time, nobody will care. You do have a unique opportunity, however, to redefine yourselves," he adds chuckling; "but not much by way of the means to do so."

"How can you do this to us?" one prisoner angrily yells from the front row.

"Feed this man pig shit," Creed instructs his guards.

The guards shove the prisoner to the ground. One of them pulls swine feces from a bucket and presses it against the man's mouth and nose, forcing shit into his mouth the moment he gasps for air. The prisoner, now in tears, begins to dry heave. The sight is sickening. Other prisoners look away, but Vandoc watches carefully, hiding all emotion, taking everything in.

"I actually welcome outbursts during my orientations," Creed yells. "These *teaching moments*, if you will, give me a chance to walk-the-walk so to speak. Now for those who wish not to dine on pig shit, repeat after me," he instructs. "I am but a piss roach in the service of the Khan," he yells.

"I AM BUT A PISS ROACH IN THE SERVICE OF THE KHAN," the prisoners begin to yell in response.

"What?" Colonel Creed yells. "I didn't hear that."

"I AM BUT A PISS ROACH IN THE SERVICE OF THE KHAN," they yell again, but more loudly and in unison.

"Barring my own craft," Creed says; "the ship that brought you here today is the only flight on or off this moon. In short, you will not be leaving here ever again. No prisoner has. There is no escape. You can, however, prolong your life here through obedience and hard work in the iridium mines. That much is up to you. I am not your enemy. You are now all subjects of the Khan, which puts us on the same team."

Guards then turn power hoses on the naked prisoners. After they are hosed down collectively, they are issued prison uniforms. As they drip dry, they are forced to drink an entire cup of a creamy blue liquid in front of armed officers. From there, they are transported directly to a mine, where they are forced to extract iridium from rock with pick axes. After a very short training, they are immediately put to work for several hours. It is only after their first full shift that they are finally assigned cells, all in accordance with the Khan's policy that prisoners sow before they reap.

Beyond exhaustion, Vandoc enters his cell to find his cellmate sitting on his bunk with eyes full of tears. Vandoc immediately recognizes him to be the man who was forced to eat the swine feces.

"They told me the guy I replaced today answered the call of Dyvok," the man tells Vandoc. "That means the volcano called to him; it means he jumped into the volcano."

"Oh, I've never heard that," Vandoc replies. "That's gotta suck."

"I'm gonna kill him. I'm going to kill that heartless fuck, I swear to it. We're gonna die here anyway, so I'm gonna kill him," the man says.

"You're Pawani,[1] aren't you?" Vandoc asks to lighten the topic.

"Yes, my name is Magnus," the man answers.

"It's good to meet you, Magnus," Vandoc says. "I'm Vandoc. Can I ask how you ended up here?"

"I voted," Magnus answers. "I voted against the Khan in a free and open election."

"That's it?" Vandoc asks.

"How about you?" Magnus asks. "How did you end up here?"

---

[1] The **Pawani**, a religious group originally from India, were the first settlers to the system, arriving centuries before the Khan and the Khanate arrived.

"I'm a pilot from Mars. I used the wrong combox in South Kublai and somehow walked out of it and into North Kublai," Vandoc answers.

"Sounds like you've been railroaded," Magnus says.

"You seem to know a lot about the Kingdom," Vandoc notes.

"What they've done to my people amounts to nothing more than the crime of the galaxy," Magnus replies.

"So do you know where we are?" Vandoc asks. "They never told us and nobody seems to know."

"We're on Pyro," Magnus answers.

"The famous moon?" Vandoc responds. He remembers reading where it had been used for a prisoner of war camp during the great conflict, but that's nothing he wants to tell Magnus. As much as he'd love to talk, mentioning any information that reveals his military background could put Magnus or himself in danger.

"You know of this moon?" Magnus asks.

"Many do," Vandoc answers. "Isn't it mentioned in the Book of Time?"

"Many times," Magnus answers; "for *Caribon* was born of this moon."

"There is a coffee shop near where I live on Mars that is called the Caribon Cafe," Vandoc says.

"I know so little of the legend. Please teach me," he requests.

"Sure, for I know much. I am a scholar of the Book of Time," Magnus says. "The legend of Caribon begins both here on the moon of Pyro and on its host planet, *Mythos*; the only naturally habitable planet in the system, and home of my ancestors. Caribon was born of both Pyro and Mythos," he adds; "during Unibon."

"The time when these two celestial bodies swing so close to each other that they almost collide," Vandoc says, aware of that much of the legend.

"Yes," Magnus says; "when the moon and planet make love. They actually share atmospheres, you know?"

"So Caribon was the product of this planetary fornication," Vandoc says with a laugh.

"Was, or will be," Magnus tells him; "but I'll get to that. You see, my people lived peacefully on Mythos for over two centuries, keeping to ourselves before those animals arrived," Magnus says, now with a distant look in his eyes. "Nobody is allowed to live on Mythos anymore, the most livable planet in the system."

"Nobody?" Vandoc asks.

"Virtually nobody, just a few farmers," Magnus answers. "It's an agrarian planet, so most work is done robotically. It's also full of quasar root fields, so forbidding visitors is pretty much the easiest way for the Kingdom to secure its commodity."

"You were an agrarian people," Vandoc notes.

"And still are," Magnus replies. "Many farms were given option to relocate to the terraformed planet of *Shangdu*, now the agricultural center of the Kingdom."

"And you say Caribon arrived on Mythos, or will arrive there, in the legend?" Vandoc asks, steering Magnus away from his pain and back to the tale.

"The Book of Time says that Caribon was born of Pyro, the moon on which we sit, and Mythos, the planet this moon orbits," Magnus says. "I'd point it out, but our cell has no windows."

"So how often does Unibon occur?" Vandoc asks.

"It happens fairly often," Magnus replies; "but not at regular intervals, due to the complex gravitational interplay of Pyro with Mytho's other moons. Every so often, Pyro gets nudged very close to Mythos."

"They really get close enough to share atmospheres?" Vandoc asks in amazement.

"Yes, they do," Magnus answers. "The sharing of atmospheres is what defines Unibon. It's also why this moon is so volcanically active. The exchange of gravity between these bodies during each close swing causes seismic activity, metals to liquify, and the surface of this moon to change violently near the point of interplay. Throughout history, countless objects have been known to cross between celestial bodies. Even piss roaches have been traced back to Mythos."

"Fascinating," Vandoc adds.

"Pyro's orbit is highly elliptical and in decay. This perpetual shift, however, presents opportunity. Persistent pockets of iridium, normally found deep beneath its lunar surface have been resurfacing. The Khan's plan is to mine iridium until this moon is tapped out, or until it breaks apart, whichever comes first."

"So, what did Caribon ultimately do?" Vandoc asks Magnus.

"He climbed down from this moon, into Mythos and freed my people," Magnus answers.

"Your people aren't free," Vandoc tells him.

"Yet, we were when the Book of Time was written," Magnus replies; "which leads to my theory."

"So, you think the tale of Caribon has yet to unravel?" Vandoc asks.

"People who tell the legend of Caribon often forget that it comes from the Book of Time, which says at its beginning that it is a record that spans all of time."

"So, you think the events in the Book of Time may have yet to transpire," Vandoc says nodding.

"Indeed, at least the latter ones. I see them as a foretelling of sorts. It's what keeps me going at least," Magnus replies.

"Do you actually believe the legend?" Vandoc asks.

"Let's say that I don't disbelieve it," Magnus answers.

"Fair enough," Vandoc says. "I'll believe it too if it sets me free."

"Legend only mentions Caribon setting the Pawani free," Magnus replies laughing. "You're on your own."

"How do you know I'm not Caribon?" Vandoc asks. They both laugh.

"Why not?" Magnus asks aloud. "A popular verse from the Book of Time often quoted in Pawani culture is *all men in every man*," he tells Vandoc, "which is to say that there is a little part of everyone in everyone. We are all of the same ilk."

"I like that," the captain replies.

"Your case is odd," Magnus tells Vandoc. "Why would they abduct a pilot from Mars?"

"Do you think this was intentional?" Vandoc asks. "Do you think they knew I was a pilot?"

"Remember, they still consider themselves at war here, and they know they're losing to the Colonies," Magnus says. "They're getting desperate. If they want you as a bargaining chip, it doesn't make sense that you are here at an undisclosed camp."

"What did they have us drink," Vandoc asks; "the blue stuff?"

"It's a blood enhancer; an isotope that trips location beacons throughout this moon, and police beacons throughout the entire system," Magnus answers. "It wears off over time. I don't know how long it takes, but prisoners have to take it twice a year. Rumor has it that sensors can detect a single drop within fifty meters, even of dried blood."

Chapter 5

"Welcome to South Kublai, Agent Sandbrook," a woman in military fatigue says with a smile. "As requested, you are docked at Berth 33 in the Neutral Zone and here are the flight manifests and footage of the crew exiting their craft has been transferred to you. Can I get you anything else?" she asks.

"Not at this time," Agent Sandbrook tells her. "I need to get to the hotel."

Twenty-one minutes later.

"Welcome to the Seasons Hotel, Mr. Sandbrook," a receptionist says with a warm smile. "As you requested, we have you in room #3391. We have also transferred the information you have requested. We hope that you enjoy your stay with us."

"Thank you," Agent Sandbrook tells them. "We're dealing with a disappearance and time may be of the essence."

"We understand," the night manager replies. "Our staff has answered all questions you submitted and are standing by to help."

"I appreciate that," the agent tells her as he collects his things and checks into the room. Once inside, he lays the information out in front of him on the bed and begins examining the case detail for detail. He starts going through collected video testimonials.

- "I remember him," one maid says. "He checked in and quickly left. I could tell because he hadn't even unpacked his toiletries, nothing."
- "Sure, I remember him checking in," another young woman says. "He had a nice smile. Anyway, he didn't have much to say. He did come back down to the lobby, I remember, because he stared out at the sea. He met another guy, too. The same guy who checked in with him."

One hour later, Agent Sandbrook sits at the bar in Microns talking to Tyban, the nightshift manager.

"So, this is all the footage you have from Christmas Eve?" Sandbrook asks, looking discouraged.

"I'm afraid so," Tyban answers, looking over the dark bar scene with the agent. "I was in the Colonial Forces, you know," Tyban tells Sandbrook.

"Really," the agent replies. "Which division?" he asks.

"I was with Sky Fleet, stationed near the galactic core," Tyban answers.

"You just never know who you'll run across, even way out here," Sandbrook replies. "It's a pleasure to meet you, soldier."

"The honor is all mine, Agent," Tyban replies. They smile and shake hands.

"Now, who is that?" Sandbrook asks, pointing to the screen. "There's someone else joining them. Have you seen him before?" he asks.

"Not that I recall," Tyban answers; "but I'll keep an eye out."

"I'd appreciate that," Agent Sandbrook responds with a smile.

"Anything for the Colonies," Tyban answers solemnly.

Chapter 6

The morning sky is clear. Mythos comes into view as Magnus and Vandoc walk into the mouth of a mighty mine. Magnus points to the sky.

"Look how close we are to it today," he tells Vandoc, pointing to Mythos.

"Damn," Vandoc says, stunned by the view.

"You think this is close," Magnus says; "wait until Unibon. See where *the Great Ocean* meets the land, about half way up?" he asks while pointing at Mythos' visible terrain.

"Yeah," Vandoc replies.

"That dry, tan area is the *Vast Flats*, mentioned in the Book of Time. It was the land of my people before the Khan took it. "There," he points; "you can trace the *Serpent River* westward. It leads to *Timeless Valley*. You're only safe on the south side of that river though," he tells Vandoc.

"Why is that?" Vandoc asks.

"Porlock," Magnus answers; known for its predatory wit, but preys only on the river's northern plain.

"Yes," Vandoc replies, staring at the planet. "I've heard of Porlock, the mighty beast."

Deep within the mine, the men are subjected to back-breaking labor and persistent mind-breaking harassment. Rumors flow among elder inmates that the suicide rate, already high, has tripled under

Colonel Creed. An estimated thirty-six percent of inmates have answered the call of Dyvok. Many cases are known to be legit, others suspicious.

Magnus and Vandoc line up with their crew.

"Good morning, roaches," their crew commander announces. "Today, tomorrow, and for the rest of your worthless existences, we'll be continuing with the de-clumping of stone. Keep your eyes out for metals." The men begin swinging pickaxes at endless piles of stone.

"Commander," Vandoc asks; "can I have a word with you?"

"Guards, seize the Martian," the commander yells.

Two guards run over, grab Captain Vandoc and shove him to his knees in front of the commander. He is then forced to lie on his stomach face down. The crew gathers around.

"This piss roach wants a word with me," the commander yells. "Well, out with it, piss roach. What is our word?"

"I wanted to ask if I could use a fon," Vandoc says face down.

"A fon, I see," the commander yells in laughter. "Of course, a fon." The commander then kicks Captain Vandoc squarely in the stomach. The crew begins to turn away. "And just who do you think you're going to call, Martian?" the commander asks.

"Nobody on Mars can help you. You're in the Kingdom. Know anybody in the Kingdom who can help? I didn't think s…"

"Maxiums Krylok," Vandoc says, wincing in pain from the kick.

"Who did you say?" the commander asks as a look of surprise overtakes his face.

"Maxiums Krylok," Vandoc says again. The captain turns and looks at his guards.

Ten minutes later, Vandoc finds himself in Creed's chambers awaiting a meeting with the Colonel.

"Kneel, Captain," the guard instructs him. "Do not look at the Colonel unless he tells you to do so."

"Understood," Vandoc tells them as he drops to a knee.

Colonel Creed enters the room with his right-hand man, Boron. The guards salute. Vandoc remains on one knee with his head bowed.

"I will speak and you will listen," Creed tells Vandoc. "You are to address me as 'My Wiser,' is that understood?"

"Yes, My Wiser," Vandoc answers.

"I am not one to pry unless matters arise which may concern me, the Khan, or the Kingdom," Creed says. "That said, when I do want answers to questions, I have a very low tolerance for dishonesty. Is that understood?"

"Yes, My Wiser," Vandoc replies.

"I have only one question for you today," Creed tells Vandoc. "Beyond piloting, what skills do you have within your skillset?" he asks.

"I am an aerospace engineer, a navigator, and an astrophysicist," Vandoc answers forthrightly.

Creed and Boron give each other a look of approval.

"You will be reassigned immediately. You will be pulled from the mines to work with my ship's maintenance crew. Your working hours will remain the same for the time being," Creed tells Vandoc. "Is that understood?" he asks.

"Yes, My Wiser," Vandoc answers, confused.

"You may begin immediately," Creed tells him.

Later that evening, back in his cell.

"Who the hell is Maxiums Krylok?" Magnus asks Vandoc as he enters their cell.

"I wish I knew," Vandoc answers. "I met the guy minutes before being abducted. Dropping his name somehow caught Creed's attention, yet didn't seem to matter to him. He still treated me like shit."

"Maybe they've yet to contact this Maxiums guy," Magnus suggests.

"God, I hope so," Vandoc responds.

"Are you going to kill him?" Magnus asks.

"Who, Krylok?" Vandoc asks.

"No, Colonel Creed," Magnus replies.

"Believe me," Vandoc answers; "I want him dead, but killing him is not my intention."

"Then what is your intention?" Magnus inquires.

"Getting out of here," Vandoc answers, lying on his bunk.

"Dream on," Magnus tells Vandoc. "Nobody leaves here. Our dreams are destined to be volcano food."

"Volcano food," Vandoc repeats with a chuckle.

"What's your rush anyway?" Magnus asks.

"I have a wife out there; a beautiful woman, waiting for me until death," Vandoc answers.

"Until death?" Magnus asks. "Are you sure?"

"It's in our wedding vows," Vandoc replies. "We wrote them ourselves."

"Fair enough," Magnus replies. "I don't mean to flip shit at you. If I sound so negative, it's because my wife didn't wait around for me."

"Sorry to hear it," Vandoc replies.

"Thanks," Magnus answers. "So, what does Creed want you to do for him?" he asks.

"He has put me to work on his private ship," Vandoc answers.

"Doing what?" Magnus asks.

"So far, I have been helping his crew with the navigation system," Vandoc answers. "I'm an engineer."

"Exercise extreme caution around Creed and bury your ego," Magnus tells him. "Your life may very well depend on it."

"I know," Vandoc replies. "God, how I wish I could go back to the mines."

Both men sit in silence.

"So, tell me more of the legend," Vandoc requests. "So Caribon descends onto the planet Mythos, after the planet screws this moon in an act known as Unibon."

"Yes," Magnus replies. "If you think we could see Mythos well this morning, wait until Unibon. During Unibon, the surface of Mythos will be all that can be seen, taking up our entire sky. Rivers, valleys, and mountains will all be rushing by at a high speed, visible but dark beneath the kiss of Mythos' shadow.

Mountains tremble and the ground shakes as waves of iron and nickel liquefy under the immense gravitational interplay. Many say an evil sound can be heard."

"So Caribon originally comes from this moon, and is sucked into Mythos during Unibon," Vandoc suggests.

"I suppose," Magnus replies, thinking.

"Then what happens;" Vandoc asks; "after Caribon descends onto the planet?"

"He makes his great pilgrimage to Timeless Valley," Magnus answers; "where he eventually leads my people to their freedom."

"What about Porlock, the legendary beast?" Vandoc asks. "Was this when he encounters Porlock, on his trek?"

"Yes," Magnus answers, before pausing again in thought. "There is no beast on Mythos known to the Pawani that remotely fits the description of the Porlock, leaving many to question if the story was literal, or merely parable," Magnus replies. "Myself, I am of the former. I fear that the beast is quite real, but most likely yet to be."

"When?" Vandoc asks. "Any estimated time of arrival?"

"No, but this moon is in a declining orbit around Mythos, destined to break apart and eventually become its next ring system. I suppose it would have to happen by then," Magnus replies.

"How does a beast evolve in that time?" Vandoc asks.

"The Khan has darker motives behind forbidding travel to Mythos to travelers than the mere protection of crops," Magnus says.

"What?" Vandoc asks.

"Abominations performed in the name of genetic science that, like this place, if known would shut down all trade between the Kingdom and the Colonies," Magnus answers. "A lot of genetic modifications have taken place on the planet. The Khan has long sought to build the perfect beast. So, the Porlock could easily already lurk for all we know."

"What does the Book of Time say about the beast?" Vandoc asks.

"It says little by way of physical description," Magnus answers. "It remains artfully vague. We do know Porlock shelters in the limestone caves beyond the flats, at the mouth of the Serpent River. He is a predator to be feared by all others. We also know that upon seeing the Porlock, one should assume to have also been seen. Porlock, however, is foul to the nose, which though unpleasant, can give its prey advantage."

"Amusing," Vandoc says staring at the ceiling. "I don't know how true any of that is, but it certainly is entertaining."

Chapter 7

A warm breeze flows through the canyon.

"You have been to Kublai and back?" Nebula asks wide-eyed.

"Does that surprise you?" Agent Sandbrook asks, sitting on a deck overlooking Mars' mighty *Valles Marineris*.

"Yes, but pleasantly," she answers. "I'm glad to hear that you're so devoted to my husband's case."

"That I am," the agent replies, slowly shaking his head and stroking his chin. "Do you mind if I ask you a few questions?"

"Absolutely," Nebula answers.

"Did your husband mention meeting or talking to anybody other than Nario Shorebok before or during his trip to Kublai?" Agent Sandbrook asks.

"No, nobody. Why?" Nebula asks.

"I found surveillance footage of your husband in a bar, talking with what appears to be Nario Shorebok and one other unidentified individual," Agent Sandbrook says.

"Really?" Nebula asks.

"It was the last place in which he was seen," Sandbrook tells her. "The bar is in an area of town known to be very Khan sympathetic. If only they knew of the atrocities that sit mere meters away. Anyway, I was just wondering who this other guy might be."

"Have you asked Nario?" Nebula asks.

"Not yet," Sandbrook answers. "It's odd that he never mentioned a third person when I interviewed him right after your husband's disappearance."

"What do you think happened to my husband?" Nebula asks.

"I don't know," Agent Sandbrook replies. "I suspect he has been kidnapped by the Kingdom."

"Why would they kidnap Vandoc?" Nebula asks.

"His expertise," Agent Sandbrook answers. "Your husband possesses rare knowledge and unique skills. When the Khan sees something that he wants, he takes it, either to put to use within his Kingdom or to use as a bargaining chip."

"So, he's alive," Nebula says.

"Very likely," Agent Sandbrook replies. "In fact, I believe he is," he adds. "I've read his file too, and if anyone can survive the Kingdom, he can."

"The Kingdom is all he ever reads about," Nebula tells the agent.

"Really?" Sandbrook asks. "That's interesting. I thank you for your time," he tells her. "Understand that we are on this case and will do everything within our power to get your husband home safely."

"Thank you, agent," Nebula replies as she sees him to the door.

Agent Sandbrook checks the time.

Chapter 8

"Something's up," Gear, the ship's lead mechanic tells Vandoc.

"What do you mean?" Vandoc asks.

"A lot of people have been showing up here lately," Gear answers; "dignitaries. Something's going on." Creed, now donning formal military wear, walks toward them, giving a small tour to two other men, also in full uniform.

"My Wiser, would you be so thoughtful as to authorize this parts manifest?" Vandoc asks Creed, showing him a holographic itemized list.

"This is Captain Piss Roach," Creed tells two men with him. They all chuckle. "He claims to know Maxiums Krylok," he adds in laughter.

"Maxiums Krylok," one of the men repeats. A serious look overtakes their faces.

"You know him," Vandoc says to the men. "Can you tell him that Captain Vandoc is here?" he pleads.

"I'll let him know, Captain" the man says; "sure."

"Thank you," Vandoc replies.

Colonel Creed escorts the men away. He soon returns, however, with two guards who grab Vandoc, force him to his knees and restrain him. Creed approaches, stares into his eyes, then swiftly slugs Vandoc, landing an excruciatingly painful abdominal punch just below his left ribcage.

"There are two things you need to understand, Captain," Creed tells Vandoc; "one, Maxiums Krylok, whoever the fuck you think he is, is not going to save you. In fact, he won't be able to do a damn thing for you. It would be within your best interest to forget about him and focus on your own survival. Two, if you ever speak out of line again, you will not only be fed but also be forced to ingest an entire bucket of pig shit," Creed adds. "Do I make myself clear?"

"Yes, My Wiser," Vandoc answers, grimacing in pain.

Vandoc soon finds himself working alone on the flight deck of the massive *Condor 5*, Creed's private ship. He logs into the navigation system. Like clockwork, the maps show Mythos approaching head on.

Vandoc runs a planetary trajectory simulation, and voila, as he suspected; Unibon. The two celestial lovers are soon to dance again. When Vandoc stops the simulation at the closest point between the two bodies, the navigation system shows something he's never seen on screen; a gravitational anomaly. The two bodies' gravitational pulls negate each other, creating a momentary region between them that shows an upper atmospheric area where g-forces not only drop to zero, but actually appear to go negative.

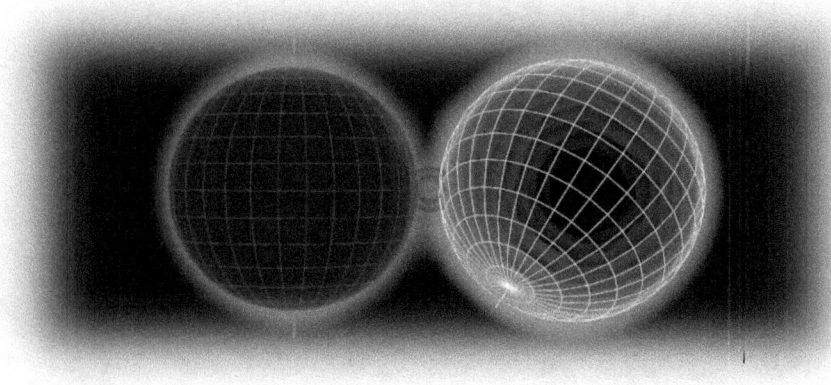

Better yet, this Unibon is to hit very close to home, geographically. In fact, Mt. Dyvok falls just within the path of Mythos' forecasted shadow. Vandoc sits back, allowing his thoughts to sink deep, then smiles.

"Something big is on the way," Vandoc tells Magnus as they lie on their bunks.

"What?" Magnus asks.

"Unibon," Vandoc answers.

"I thought I felt the southerly winds, the winds of warning, coming through the canyons," Magnus replies. "How do you know it's Unibon?" he asks.

"I ran a simulation on the navigation computer on Creed's ship," Vandoc answers. "It's coming in nine days."

"I thought I remembered the calendars mentioning something around this time," Magnus replies. "So that's why all of Creed's military asshats have been around."

"We're going to have a front row seat," Vandoc adds. "This one is close to home. Dyvok is in its path."

"You know this?" Magnus asks.

"I know this," Vandoc answers.

"Creed won't stay here," Magnus tells Vandoc.

"Why not?" Vandoc asks.

"They know this moon is unstable," Magnus answers. "Whenever it does finally break apart, it will occur during Unibon."

"Taking us out with it," Vandoc says.

"That part they love," Magnus replies. "What better way to rid themselves of any evidence of this illegal facility?"

"So how much danger do we face?" Vandoc asks.

"Unibon has collapsed entire valleys, twisted mountains, and caused mighty quakes," Magnus replies. "This moon's largest canyon was cut during Unibon just a decade ago. So, who knows?"

"Where will they go?" Vandoc asks.

"Who?" Magnus asks.

"Creed and these guys you called assholes," Vandoc answers.

"Asshats," Magnus replies. "I called them asshats. Anyway, they'll probably go to Mythos, where they can observe the event from a safer location. It's only off limits to the general public, not military brass. They oversee security for the planet anyway. They have a port there that they use as a luxury resort. Not a lot of security is required on a planet that forbids access to the public."

"How sure are you that Creed will leave?" Vandoc asks.

"Absolutely," Magnus answers.

Vandoc lies in his bed, phased as his mind begins to beget a profoundly unique plan. This is real, no longer hypothetical. A thousand thoughts race through his mind as he lies in silence. He knows himself too well. The dots are all there. He has, however, only nine days to connect them.

Vandoc also knows he can no longer speak openly. His thoughts are now dangerous, and to divulge any of them to Magnus, Gear, or anyone he trusts would be to turn them into accomplices. Lie-detection would sniff them out under interrogation. They could easily be executed. Vandoc knows he is truly on his own with this one.

"Creed punched me," Vandoc tells Magnus. "My ribs are killing me."

"That fuck," Magnus replies. "What set him off?" he asks.

"I spoke out of line," Vandoc answers. "He mentioned the name Maxiums Krylok to his fellow officers. I had to ask if they knew who he was."

"What did they say?" Magnus asks.

"One of them said that he would tell Krylok I'm here," Vandoc answered.

"Do you believe him?" Magnus asks.

"No, frankly," Vandoc answers. "I don't know. If Maxiums Krylok is who he said he was, and these guys know him, or at least of him, why am I still being treated like an animal?"

"Maybe they don't believe you really know him," Magnus suggests.

"Who knows?" Vandoc replies. "If that's the case, I hope they contact Krylok."

"You also have to wonder if this guy, Krylok, had anything to do with you being here," Magnus adds.

A long moment of silence ensues as both men ponder the thought.

"I heard the call of Dyvok today," Vandoc says.

"Are you sure?" Magnus asks somberly.

"The call was faint but clear," Vandoc answers.

"Perhaps it was just momentary," Magnus replies; "fleeting."

"Perhaps," Vandoc responds; "perhaps."

Chapter 9

Interstellar freight-liners arrive, one after another, docking just long enough to unload and reload. The red planet, seen from Mars Dock, an orbital station high above, is breathtaking. Agent Sandbrook pauses for a moment in Docking Bay 9 to take it in.

"Agent Sandbrook, I must say I'm a bit surprised to see you here," Nario says as the agent enters his office. "How are things progressing with Captain Vandoc's case?" he asks.

"Well," Sandbrook replies; "and I really hate to barge in on people at their places of work, but this was the place from which you and Captain Vandoc departed. In my line of work, I've learned to simply take in as many details as possible, whether they turn out to have any relevance or not."

"Interesting," Nario replies.

"I think so as well," Sandbrook tells him. "It can be tedious, and most information turns out to lack relevance," he adds; "but you never know what fact might crack a case."

"What do you think has happened to Captain Vandoc?" Nario asks.

"I'm convinced that he's in the Kingdom," Sandbrook answers; "and not of his own accord."

"Who could have forced him into the Kingdom?" Nario asks.

"A number of people on a short list," Agent Sandbrook answers; "which leads me to a question I wanted to ask you."

"Absolutely, Agent," Nario replies.

"Last time we spoke, you told me that you and Captain Vandoc were alone in the lounge on the night he disappeared," Sandbrook notes.

"Yes, we were," Nario replies.

"Well, I've been to the lounge, Microns," Sandbrook says. "I saw footage from the restaurant that shows you, Captain Vandoc, and someone else in the lounge, having a discussion."

"Are you certain it was us?" Nario asks.

"Quite," Sandbrook answers.

"Oh yes, I remember us chatting with some guy very briefly," Nario says. "I wouldn't say we had much of a conversation."

"What was his name?" the agent asks.

"I didn't ask and I don't remember him volunteering it," Nario responds.

"Do you smell that?" Sandbrook asks.

"Smell what?" Nario asks in return.

"I thought I smelled something," Sandbrook replies. "Sorry, anyway, what did you guys talk about?" he asks.

"Nothing really," Nario answers, looking bewildered. "He just asked where we were from and what brought us to Kublai."

"Can you describe him?" Sandbrook asks.

"He was pale, taller, and somewhat thin. His hair was blonde, but white around the temples," Nario says, looking less confident as the interview continues.

"Thank you for your time today," Agent Sandbrook tells him. "I'll get out of your hair and let you get back to work."

"Thank you, agent," Nario responds. "Do you think you'll find him?"

"I do," Sandbrook answers. "You see, Captain Vandoc was more valuable than civilians know or understand for that matter. If it's determined he was taken, he may easily become a bargaining chip, we may find him, or he may find his way out of the Kingdom."

"How could he ever find his own way out?" Nario asks.

"That, I wish I could tell you," Sandbrook answers. "Revealing what I know on this topic would violate the terms of my security clearance. I can say, however, though a statistical improbability, getting out of the Kingdom alive is a possibility; and from what I know of Captain Vandoc, I wouldn't bet against him."

Chapter 10

Back on Pyro, the day of Unibon has dawned. Magnus and Vandoc sit silently on a prison transport pod. The dread of another day in the mines, knowing he'll miss Unibon, weighs on Magnus' face. These asshats, he thinks, won't even tell the prisoners what has now become quite obvious; that Unibon is upon us, and coming to this valley. The mines could easily collapse and are the last place anyone should be. The Khan, the Kingdom, Creed, they just don't care.

"Are you sure Creed will leave?" Vandoc asks again.

"I'd say about ninety-seven, point four percent," Magnus answers.

"You were a hundred percent certain last night," Vandoc says.

"Why do you care?" Magnus asks.

"I guess I'm just sick of seeing his face," Vandoc answers.

The pod pulls out of an underground tunnel, onto the surface of Pyro. Powerful, howling winds immediately whip, shaking it violently. The men look out of an overhead window at a sight that leaves them speechless; Mythos has risen and now covers nearly half of the entire sky. Soon, there will be no sky. It already looks like it should be colliding with this moon, but depth can be deceiving when face to face with a ball that size.

"Holy God of the Gardens," Magnus says. "My home has come to me."

"I only see blue," Vandoc says, looking up to see nothing but water beneath Mythos' partly cloudy sky.

"We're facing the Great Sea right now," Magnus answers. "God, how I wish I could at least watch it go by," he says as the pod pulls into his station at the entrance to the mines.

The Legendary Escape of Captain Vandoc

"Stay safe," Vandoc tells him, knowing down inside he may never see Magnus again.

"You too," Magnus says, looking somewhat puzzled as he gets off the pod. "Don't do anything foolish," he yells to Vandoc as the pod pulls away in the blustery wind.

Dark music plays over the sound system as Vandoc arrives at Creed's quarters to find Creed slouched in his command chair. He has a topless woman at each side. Both women are clad only in thongs and military hats, kneeling, resting their heads on Creed's thighs. There are two of Creed's fellow officers in the chamber as well, each with an alluring maiden by his side. They appear to have been drinking all night. Relieved Creed hasn't left Pyro yet, Vandoc approaches him with one last parts order to sign. Creed, on the verge of passing out, looks over a hologram of the list. Vandoc looks on nervously.

"I'm busy piss roach," Creed tells Vandoc, reeking of alcohol.

"Very well, My Wiser," Vandoc responds. "I just didn't want to delay your ship upgrades."

"Get on your knees," Creed tells Vandoc. Vandoc drops to his knees. "This piss roach has an attitude," Creed tells his guests. "He says what he's supposed to, but you can see it in his eyes. He has not been broken, yet." Creed's friends laugh. "You will break, roach, or you will die," he adds. He signs the parts order. "You may dwell on this as you take your leave, Captain," he says to Vandoc before spitting on him.

"Yes, My Wiser," Vandoc replies as he climbs to his feet. He gives Colonel Creed a slight obligatory bow and leaves the room.

Captain Vandoc retreats to a remote section of Creed's hanger, as far away from Creed as he can get. There, he bides his time pretending to work while staring at monitors, wondering why Creed hasn't left this moon. His stress is growing by the minute. Another gust of wind shakes the entire hanger as Mythos rolls closer yet. Time is ticking.

"I want to kill that son of a bitch," Vandoc says to an empty room. "Magnus had his priorities straight. I should just kill him; put him out of his misery."

Creed's ship sits motionless in the hanger.

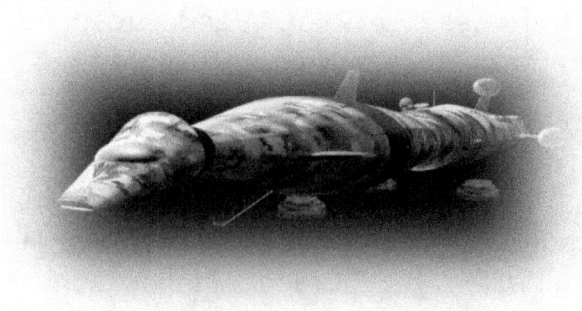

"Why in God's name is that bastard still here?"

Forcing the Captain to drop to his knees like a circus monkey was the final straw. It has come to this. There is no other way. It was just the incentive Vandoc needed to follow through with his gutsy plan. His plan, however, hinges on Creed's departure from this God-forsaken moon, and happening within the next eight minutes in order for Vandoc to make his window.

Creed can be heard laughing in the distance. Vandoc checks the time. "That fuck," he utters to himself. Then he hears it coming from Creed's hanger; his ship is firing up. They are leaving. Vandoc laughs in anticipation as he looks at the time. Creed's ship lifts off the pad, angles forward, and slowly glides above Pyro's surface before lifting into the sky.

Vandoc checks the time. He is two minutes behind his own estimated abort-mission point. There is no time to think, only act. Decisively, he makes a b-line for the parts room. Inside, he wastes no time getting into an emergency jump suit. He straps on survival packs. He then runs into Creed's chambers and starts stuffing the pockets of his jumpsuit with all remaining square root left over from Creed's drunken Unibon pre-funk.

An evil shriek is heard as metal bends under great gravitational force beneath Pyro's surface. Unibon is happening. Again, Vandoc checks the time, now three minutes behind. He runs down a central corridor to Loading Bay 4, where he has a duffle bag packed and ready. He picks it up and leaves Creed's chambers through a side exit.

Once outside, he has to stop in awe of a sight that would drop anyone to their knees. Mythos now occupies the entire sky. It's dark out. Vandoc feels something he hasn't felt in some time; alive. He's witnessing forces far greater than he could have ever conjured. The wind whips violently through the valley as again the loud, horrible sound of bending iron echoes like a ship's hull cracking in two before sinking. It's frightening and unbearable. Unibon is not a beautiful act of love. It's destructive and violent.

Vandoc is four minutes behind schedule by the time he arrives at Side Bay 3. He's losing time. His gear is weighing him down. He pauses to make one final judgement. He has been recorded, but only in Creed's chambers with everybody gone, on video files that will likely never be viewed. Once he takes the next step, however, he'll cross the Rubicon. Unfortunately, he has no time to think.

"I can't kneel to that sick fuck again," he says aloud to himself. "I just can't. I can't."

Vandoc, weighed down by his own gear and now five minutes behind, looks around for a *helium hoist*; a balloon like bag that can be filled with compressed helium and used to suspend or carry heavy parts. He had hoped one would be inflated and ready to take, but finds none. Fate is toying with him. Then he spots one floating behind an outboard thruster. What luck. Not having to fill a hoist gets three of his lost minutes back.

Vandoc straps his bag to the hoist, then tethers himself to the balloon with an expandable micro-carbon cable that connects to the belt of his suit. Nervous but excited, he looks around. It's hard to believe that nobody is watching him. He hits a green button and the bay doors open. He guides the helium hoist by tether through the door. It's huge. Once the balloon is outside, he runs back into the loading bay to close the bay doors, which he has to run through yet again to get back outside before they close. He wants to leave no trace; no reason to suspect anything unusual went down here.

The unpredictable winds make guiding the helium hoist a challenge, sometimes lifting Vandoc off his feet. There is something divine in the winds, however, for they not only lift the captain, but carry him as well, straight toward his intended destination, Mt. Dyvok. This divine wind not only makes up for lost time, but puts Vandoc one minute ahead of his dreaded cut off. Now, however, there is no going back.

Using an air compressor to steer the hoist, Captain Vandoc manages to stay on course, hugging the conical slope, tripping every location beacon along

the common path to the rim of the volcano, as planned. Mt. Dyvok is angry today. No natural light remains. The day is as night. Above, Mythos' Great Sea is crystal clear. It's disorienting to look up at it, a massive sea in the overhead sky. The air grows thinner and gravity weaker as Vandoc turns a valve to allow more helium into the hoist. It expands further, now the size of a small craft. Would he go unnoticed in the dark? He connects his suit harness directly to the main frame of the hoist as he steers the hoist up the volcano's side, hovering just above its most trodden path. The scene is surreal.

Reaching the top of Dyvok, the captain can see into its rim. It's raging, spewing lava and spitting massive fireballs of pumice in all directions. He tries to steer dangerously closer, needing to trip the highest location beacon on the mount for his plan to be airtight. He doesn't get as close to the rim as he had hoped, however, and continues to rise, missing the final beacon. It would be futile to try to get back to the rim now. He looks up at majestic Mythos and is mind-blown that this is really happening. His hoist is now the size of a house as the helium continues to expand. Higher, the captain rises.

Details on Pyro's surface fade below as those on Mythos come into clearer view. Vandoc can feel his weight fade as the hoist slows its climb. The air is thinning. The captain pulls a helmet from his pack and puts it on, then locks it to his suit's collar ring. He activates the suit's oxygen. Above him, he can see air escaping into Mythos' atmosphere. He's so close. His hoist, however, has reached its maximum altitude, no longer capable of climbing. Vandoc unleashes himself from the hoist, opens a valve to release helium and sends it drifting back to Pyro, steering it in the direction of Dyvok, toward what he hopes to be a fiery grave. To his surprise, he discovers that he is weightless. He laughs as he does a few acrobatic maneuvers, culminating in a *Vitruvian Man* pose,[2] perfectly aligned between two worlds. The captain's eyes well as he takes the moment in, for never has he felt such bliss.

---

[2] **Vitruvian Man**: famous drawing by Leonardo da Vinci, dated to c. 1490. Inspired by the writings by the ancient Roman architect Vitruvius. The drawing depicts a naked man within a circle and a square.

Lapsing time pulls him back to reality, however; back to the incredible danger he now faces. He grabs hold of the air compression canister and begins steering himself further toward Mythos. It works, he finds, as he can see himself moving away from the hoist. The canister, however, soon loses pressure and he begins to slow.

"Fuck!" he yells, staring into Mythos' beautiful blue sky. "It's right fucking there." He tries swimming but remains in place. "Son of a bitch." The window is closing and unless he can pick up some speed, he now seems destined to fall back to Pyro.

With nothing to lose, Vandoc connects his micro-carbon tether to the compressed air canister. He turns on the air and hurls it in the direction of Mythos. It begins stretching his tether as it fades into what appears to be infinity. Just before the canister disappears into Mythos' atmosphere, the cable tightens, then suddenly loosens again. It has reached the end of its elasticity, causing it to recoil. All remaining hope drains from Vandoc's face. Then he notices that the cable has tightened again. A moment later, he can see that he's moving further and further from the hoist, in Mythos' direction. "It's working!" he yells. The canister has entered Mythos' gravitational field and is now gaining weight as it begins to fall, pulling weightless Vandoc toward it. The worlds now seem to be moving apart, less aligned, yet it is Pyro that now seems to be moving away. Vandoc can barely even make out Mt. Dyvok. He laughs.

"Good fucking riddance, Creed," he yells; "asshat."

The captain soon finds himself falling toward Mythos at a high velocity, which only dawns on him as he enters the planet's upper oxygen layer. Unprepared for the shock, the captain gets knocked around like a rag doll upon entering the thickening air, almost tearing his left shoulder out of its socket. He struggles to gain control of his dive, then detaches the cable from the canister. It is only a hindrance now. He spreads his arms and legs to utilize the suit's squirrel-webbing. It wasn't designed for atmospheric entry, however, and the captain's descent remains radically out of control. Wincing in excruciating shoulder pain, he strains to regain that control.

Looking down, he sees the Great Sea, much brighter now as Genghis' natural light sheds between the two worlds. Vandoc has to squint to see but can make out land on the very distant horizon. It's the Great Continent's eastern seaboard. He's completely off target of his projected planetary entry. He tries to steer himself toward the land, but has such little control over his fall. The sea grows closer.

The captain finally manages to gain moderate control. Without the luxury of an altimeter, he eyeballs the horizon and pulls his ripcord. A chute streams from the pack on his back but fails to open.

"For the sake of fuck, what now?" he yells, just before disappearing into a cloud.

Emerging from the cloud, waves can now be seen on the sea's surface. Vandoc knows he's going to hit water, and he knows it will kill him if he can't get his chute open. He falls further and further by the second, desperately pulling on the ropes of his chute as the planet grows larger. The water's surface is now all he can see. Vandoc closes his eyes and tries to straighten his body for impact. Expecting to hit the sea's surface any second. The chute suddenly pops open. Its Silicon cords cause an immediate bounce, one that ultimately saves Vandoc's life. Far too low for safety, however, he still slams into the sea at a high speed. The impact sends him well under water and entangles him within his chute. He struggles to free himself, as the sinking chute pulls him deeper and deeper. Extreme pressure builds, threatening implosion. With all the strength he can muster, the captain manages to disconnect the suit from the chute. Exhausted of all energy, he begins to swim for the surface.

Once he makes it to the water's crest, he pulls off his helmet and sucks in the deepest breath of his life. He then looks around but sees only water. He pulls a small rubber hose attached to the collar of his suit and begins blowing into it as he struggles to stay afloat. Soon, inner rings built into the suit inflate around his ankles, knees, waist, wrists, and the back of his neck, giving him complete buoyancy. Exhausted, the captain rolls onto his back and floats beneath Mythos' endless blue sky, still half occupied by Pyro. In pain but finally relaxed, Vandoc smiles, adrift in the middle of nowhere.

"So, what did you do for Unibon this year?" he yells laughing.

Chapter 11

Creed's ship swoons through a thick cloud layer, then levels over a rocky, baron, desolate plain on its final approach into the camp.

"Welcome back Colonel," Boron says as Creed enters his chambers.

"So, what have these criminals been up to?" Creed asks, exhausted and hung over.

"Tunnel Nine collapsed, killing three prisoners," Boron answers.

"When can we clear it?" Creed asks with no regard for the prisoners.

"It will take several weeks," Boron replies.

"Anything else?" Creed asks, scratching his head.

"Captain Vandoc, Sir," Boron says.

"What about Captain Roach?" Creed asks.

"It would seem he has offed himself," Boron answers.

"What in fuck's name?" Creed yells after a moment of thought. "I didn't see that coming."

"You were pretty rough on him just before you left," Boron tells him.

"Was I?" Creed asks. "Have you informed Central Command?"

"Not yet," Boron answers. "It's the second time in a month," Boron tells him. They are going to wonder what's up."

"Fuck Central Command," Creed says.

"There's just one odd thing about the captain's suicide," Boron adds.

"What's that?" Creed asks.

"He didn't trip the top beacon on Dyvok," Boron answers.

"Hmm," Creed says, again caught in thought; "he probably got off the path and approached the rim from the northern side."

"But why would he do that?" Boron asks.

"Who knows what goes through a guy's mind before killing himself?" Creed asks. The northern rim gives a jumper an unobstructed leap into the lava. He was probably just making sure to get the job done right."

"It's just that nobody has ever done that," Boron says.

"Well now someone has," Creed responds. "Now, what happened to all the q-root we had around here?" he asks. "Could we have possibly blown through all of it?"

"I don't know, sir," Boron responds. "You know I never touch the stuff."

"You know, Boron," Creed replies; "you aren't particularly likable."

Chapter 12

"Until death do I commit to you, mind, body and soul," Nebula says through her white wedding veil, looking deeply into Vandoc's eyes.

The oxygen meter on the captain's mask drops from 1% ozone to 0% as his body sways lifelessly with the tide as it continues being pushed, wave by wave, against stones that line a rocky shoreline. The lack of oxygen brings him to. Frantically, he unlatches his helmet, gasping for air.

"Where the …" he yells; "Christ," as he rips his helmet off.

Exhausted, the captain rises to his feet. His shoulder is cut and bleeding. He sits on the shore dressing his wound, looking up at Pyro as it grows smaller, fading further into his new sky. Shivering in the cold, he is soon able to get the bleeding to stop. He rises to his feet and begins following the shoreline southward. "I've truly done it," he thinks with a smile. He now, however, has only twelve days to get to Timeless Valley, and judging by how cold the air is, he is further North than he had hoped to be.

Captain Vandoc walks for hours, following a coastline of unforgiving terrain. The rocks, sand, and cliffs are very earth-like. The trees, however, are enormous and mushroom shaped, unlike any the captain has ever seen. Mythos' gravity is nine percent stronger than Pyro's and the captain can feel it. Pyro continues to fade into a now graying sky. With the sun nearing the horizon and what looks like a storm brewing, Vandoc decides to seek shelter for his first night on the planet.

He follows a small stream inland, where he finds a semi-covered rock enclosure. There, he takes off his packs and gathers some wood. Using a laser fire starter, he is able to quickly ignite some kindling. Soon, he has a crackling fire going. He fills his only water bottle with water from the stream, then puts a purification pellet in it, one of a very limited number. He has to find other ways of getting purified water, and soon. He pulls a small solar panel from his pack

and begins charging his suit's helmet. He opens a
ready-made meal. His pack has only fifteen. Again,
he is going to have to adapt fast or perish. At least
I'm not going to die in a goddamn volcano, he thinks
with a smile.

Night falls on Mythos. For Vandoc, on the run, alone
on a forbidden planet, light years from home,
darkness has never run deeper. He hears what
sounds to be a long howl in the distance. What beast
could that be? A chill moves down his spine. This
planet doesn't support wildlife, he thinks to himself.
Soon, another howl, even closer, then another. As
the howling increases, the towering trees just outside
the captain's rock den begin to sway. A quick, cold
wind through the den makes the fire shimmy. It's the
approaching storm that howls tonight, Vandoc
realizes as he lies beside his humble fire.

Chapter 13

At Creed's feet, Magnus lies prostrate with his face to
the ground. He is shaking.

"Rise Pawani piss roach," Creed instructs.
"You look familiar," Creed says to Magnus as he
looks over his trembling face. "Where do I remember
you from?" he asks.

"I do not know, sir," Magnus replies, unwilling to even look at Creed.

"Do you recognize him?" Creed asks Boron, who only shrugs his shoulders. "Anyway," Creed says; "that's neither here nor there. I have summoned you here because your cellmate has committed suicide."

"Dear God, I'm dreadfully sorry to hear this," Magnus says.

"Are you surprised to learn of this?" Creed asks Magnus.

"Only somewhat," Magnus responds. "He has, after all, not been around in days."

"Had he spoken of suicide?" Creed asks.

"He had, sir," Magnus answers; "on one occasion."

"Oh," Creed asks. "What exactly did he say?"

"He merely said that he had heard the call of Dyvok," Magnus answers. "Nothing more. I did not ask, and he did not elaborate."

"Very well," Creed tells Magnus. "That is all for now. You may take your leave."

As Magnus nears the large metallic chamber doors, Creed calls out once again to him.

"Oh, piss roach," he yells; "it just dawned on me where I've seen your face. The pig shit," he screams as he laughs uncontrollably. "You ate pig shit upon your arrival."

Magnus exits the room clinching his fists as Creed continues to split his sides in laughter.

Chapter 14

Vandoc awakens to falling snow. It has blanketed the ground. He has slept in his survival suit, comfortably padded by the same built-in inflatable rings that he used for floatation. Fortunately, the rock enclosure he discovered has managed to keep him dry. His fire, however, exhausted itself hours ago. He's shivering cold and the wet snow has made gathering firewood a daunting task. He rubs his aching shoulder. With no idea how far north he has landed, and now only ten days to get to Timeless Valley, the captain decides to press onward. Besides, what better way to get warm than to get moving?

Vandoc follows the coastline all morning, afternoon, and into the evening. His journey leads him out of the snow, between sharp, rocky cliffs, along sandy white beaches, eventually into an endless forest of massive trees that lie on an ancient seabed of white, pink, and purple stone. The ground is arid and devoid of any vegetation, barring the trees, which, though very much alive, look dead and petrified.

As night falls, Captain Vandoc looks for firewood. It is impossible to find. The trees about him provide the only wood around but they leave nothing on the ground to gather and are far too big to climb. At least this night is calm and warmer. The skies are clear and the sun, Genghis, is going down. The first star appears, then the second. Soon the sky is sparkling with diamonds. The captain lies back in awe. Looking out over the seabed around him, he sees that the desert is aglow in pink and purple light, as far as the eye can see.

"Of course," Vandoc says to himself; "the Crystal Desert." Magnus has pointed this out on more than one occasion. The seabed is covered in hackmanite, a natural stone that emits luminescence under dark conditions. To think, he just saw this desert while standing on Pyro. Now here he is, in the center of it.

He can now also approximate his position on this planet and knows that he is at least two-hundred kilometers off his predicted course. This puts him just within his window of opportunity, and his window of survival. If he can maintain pace, he'll reach Timeless Valley on schedule, and if all goes according to plan, get the hell off this planet. With Mythos' faster spin, however, and a less than accurate touchdown on this planet, the days are too short to travel only by day. Vandoc knows he'll have to also travel by night, reducing his rests. He has enough water purification pellets, but even rationed at one a day, he's a few meals shy of reaching his destination. The further south he gets, the more plentiful plant life should be. This is, after all, an agricultural planet. The captain, nevertheless, has wagered his life on his own wits navigating him through whatever lies ahead; the unknown.

Tired and shoulder aching, the captain presses on, into the night, across a glowing seabed of light.

Chapter 15

Creed soaks in a simulated pond beneath a small waterfall, amidst three giggling damsels. They massage his temples and shoulders as ambient music softly fills the private chamber.

"Colonel," Boron's voice comes over the com.

"Why are you interrupting my spa, Boron?" Creed asks.

"A patrol just reported finding a helium hoist way out on the lava flats," Boron tells him.

"And that is why you have interrupted my bath?" Creed asks.

"It came from Loading Bay 3," Boron says.

"This Loading Bay 3?" Creed asks. "From this chamber?"

"It's marked so, and the mechanics confirm they're missing one," Boron answers.

"Interrogate all of them under lie detection," Creed instructs. "Get to the bottom of how this could happen. Someone must know something."

"Yes sir," Boron responds.

Chapter 16

On his sixth day afoot, Captain Vandoc enters a lush valley abounding with vegetation. At the mouth of the valley, on a foothill sit the stone ruins of an ancient Pawani settlement. If only Magnus could see this, the captain thinks. Lining both sides of the main path into the ruins are various fruit trees that were planted by early settlers. Several of them still bear fruit. For the first time since his capture, Vandoc is able to truly indulge. He sits on a stone overlooking the sunny coastline, eating bananas. Looking out over the ocean, he notices an island in the distance.

"That has to be the Isle of Hope," he says. "I'll be goddamned if that isn't it," he screams before taking a big bite of his banana. "That has to be it. What else could it be?" He laughs, delighted at the discernable landscape and another object he's already seen from this planet's largest moon. He knows of the historical significance of this place too. The Pawani landed on the Isle of Hope after decades in space, centuries before the Khan, long before hylo-travel speeds were even attainable.

The climate has changed and the afternoon is warm. Vandoc strips out of his suit and prison clothes to bathe himself in a brook that flows through the ancient village. The water is cold. He uses mud and sand from the bank as makeshift soap to exfoliate his funk-ridden skin. Tempted, he refrains from washing his prison clothes out of fear they won't be dry enough by nightfall, leaving him to freeze.

The captain dresses, then scavenges the village for any usable items. He is fortunate to find a few ancient but useful household items among the ruins, including a small pot for cooking or boiling water. These things must be over a thousand years old, he thinks. They aided early settlers, and now they will aid an innocent man on the run. Their legacy is fascinating, but tragically fated by the arrival of the Khan. Vandoc ponders the thought.

As night drops, so does the temperature. The captain takes shelter in an ancient Pawani home, or at least what's left of it. Its frame is dilapidated and interior filthy, but the captain has never felt more at home.

Exhausted, he lies on his back and looks out at the clear night sky full of distant stars. If only he could see Sol, Mars, and into their condo on the cliff. Even if there were a direct line of sight and ample magnification, he'd be viewing events that occurred over sixty-one thousand years ago. It's hard to grasp the complete reality of hyper-light travel. A gust of wind rattles the ancient dwelling as the captain closes his eyes.

Chapter 17

Nebula enters the *Cliff-Dweller Bistro* to find it packed with patrons looking to take in the midday view of Mars' galactically renowned canyon. There's something about the sun at its peak that really brings the ruddy rust out of the rocks. The view is jaw dropping. On the terrace, she finds Agent Sandbrook sitting at a table, talking with Inspector Perry.

"Please, have a seat," Agent Sandbrook tells Nebula as he motions for her to occupy the only remaining empty chair at the table. She does so.

"What is this about?" Nebula asks the agent, looking surprised.

"I had to travel here on unrelated matters and I thought I'd update you on your husband's case," Sandbrook tells her.

"Absolutely," Nebula answers. "I'm just a little surprised to see investigators willing to volunteer information. I'm very thankful nonetheless."

"We're all on the same team and here to help each other," Sandbrook replies.

"I appreciate that," Nebula says, a little choked up. "Now, have you learned anything new?" she asks.

"There was definitely a third guy at the bar the night your husband disappeared, chatting with your husband and Nario Shorebok," Agent Sandbrook tells her. "How well do you trust Nario Shorebok?" he then goes on to ask Nebula.

"I trust him a lot," she answers. "I've known him all my life," she snaps back defensively. She then pauses. "You don't think he'd have anything to do with my husband's disappearance, do you?" she asks with a panicked look on her face.

"I don't think anything at the moment," Agent Sandbrook answers. "I'm just collecting the pieces to a puzzle which has yet to reveal an image. I do believe, however, that it will," he adds. "That's what keeps me going."

"Has it revealed any image at all?" Nebula asks.

"Glimpses," Agent Sandbrook answers. "Just glimpses."

Chapter 18

Vandoc wakes to a distant howl in a violent wind storm. That wasn't the wind, he thinks. He wipes sweat from his drenched brow. He isn't feeling well. Looking out the window of this ancient dwelling, into the darkness, he sees pairs of eyes along the treeline, reflecting light, dozens of them. Beasts apparently do roam this planet, and the captain has drawn their interest.

Then he feels it; the first of what is to be a long night of kicks to the stomach, causing him to double over in pain. Within moments, the second kick is felt. Without warning, the captain vomits. Seconds later, he heaves again. His body is rejecting the bananas.

As the night deepens, Vandoc's health rapidly declines. Though shivering cold, he's forced to climb out of his suit, his only warmth and protection, and onto an ancient toilet, where he sits curled in pain. Sweating profusely, he covers his stomach with both hands and stares at the chicken skin on his arms. "Just leave me," he yells. "I don't care, where. Just get out of me!" Dehydration, however, has left nothing in him to come out. Tears squeeze from his eyes and roll down the sides of his face as his kick-to-the-stomach sensations continue.

Helpless, Vandoc curls in a corner near the toilet, listening to the howling wind, watching a piss roach cross the floor. Hours pass. A new day dawns, then comes to pass, yet the captain remains motionless, bathed in sweat, fading in and out of consciousness. Deep into his second night, he hears Nebula call his name. "Jonathan," she can be heard calling in the wind; "Jonathan!"

"Nebula," the captain answers, opening his eyes and raising his head to an empty room. He lays his head back down and starts to fade.

"Jonathan," Nebula calls. The captain opens his eyes again to see her in the room with him. "Jonathan, it's okay."

"What's okay?" the captain asks.

"It's okay to die," Nebula tells him, smiling sympathetically.

"Will you know I tried?" he asks her. Nebula smiles.

Chapter 19

"The Khan is pleased," Krylok tells Nario as they sit opposite each other in a crowded Kublai market. "Your debt is repaid. Once clear of the Neutral Zone, a crew will load an extra case of root on your ship. The Khan wants to show his gratitude."

"Look, this guy was more connected with Colonial Forces than I knew," Nario tells Krylok. His eyes are distant and face full of fear. "They're really looking into this, riding my ass. What if they find out? Or find him for Christ's sake?"

"Relax! Nobody comes back from where your captain went," Krylok replies in laughter. "Why are you so worried?"

"I didn't expect these guys to pry so hard," Nario answers. "He's more valuable than Nebula led me to believe."

"I'm going to tell you something that I was not planning on telling you before," Krylok says. "I'm fairly confident your captain is no longer with us, if you know what I'm saying."

"This is no time for innuendo," Nario says. "Are you saying he's dead?"

"I believe so," Krylok replies.

"How can you be so certain?" Nario asks.

"When you've been doing this as long as I have, well never mind. I just know. Anyway, the same party that took the captain has put out the same request again. This all too often means that something went wrong, so now they're looking for a replacement."

"If he's dead, no one must ever find out," Nario says, not even his wife, ever!"

"No one will," Krylok tells Nario. "You just have to do nothing. Remain composed. Let them dig all they want. They aren't going to find anything."

"What if he escaped?" Nario asks. "What if that's why they're replacing him?"

"I was told that no one has ever escaped from where he was sent, nor even returned," Nario replies.

Chapter 20

A piss roach climbs across the captain's lifeless face. He awakens and brushes the insect away. Slowly, he arises. Weak and shivering cold, he builds a fire in an ancient Pawani stone fireplace. Whatever microbe wiped him out, hadn't killed him. Could he now be immune? It wasn't worth another shot at the bananas to find out. He heats water over the fire and uses it to clean himself and his clothes.

Pyro rises in the morning sky, clearly getting closer again. Though not on a Unibon cycle, it will draw nearer yet. The captain sits by the fire's side throughout the morning, drying clothes and regaining strength, now pushing his timeline to make Timeless Valley. If his calculations are correct, he's within two days of reaching the Serpent River. From there, it's possible to make Timeless Valley in three.

When his clothes are finally dry to the touch, the captain packs what he can take, waves at Pyro up in the sky, and sets off once again.

Vandoc walks all day, now aware of where he is on the planet, at least roughly. Picking Magnus' brain has paid off. He is now following what's known in Pawani history as the *Pioneer Way*, a path that settlers first blazed over a thousand years ago. The day grows hot as the captain crosses a valley full of Poplar trees. The trees, like most of the vegetation here, can trace their ancestry to Earth. Traces of the Pawani lie everywhere, including periodic ancient petroglyphs depicting their early ships, villages, and ceremonies.

Vandoc discovers apple trees planted along the way. He picks a few and puts them in his pack, hungry, but not enough to chance it. Feeling stronger by the hour, he carries on through a blue forest, through a maze of massive mounds, and across salt flats, remnant of an ancient sea.

By late afternoon, the terrain changes. The region is much drier. Red rock and sandstone stretch as far as the eye can see. The Serpent River can't be far now. As the captain walks through a large fissure, he hears something; a rumbling of sorts. It is coming from behind him, growing. Adrenalin runs down his spine, as he quickly hides in a limestone cave within the walls of the crevice. Soon, a pack of wild skydeer run by. Vandoc smiles at the beautiful creatures as they gracefully flow like a wave over a fallen tree trunk in front of him, all focused straight ahead. Colonial Intelligence has long believed the skydeer to be extinct, an apparent miscalculation on their part.

Vandoc decides to follow the trail of the deer, at least as far as he can track it. He soon encounters a fork in the canyon with a sign apparently warning him to avoid the path leading right. Not one to question the wisdom of the ancients, he follows the leftward path. The path takes him through another small fissure. A petroglyph depicts hunters running from a massive beast with a ferocious look in its face. Of course, Vandoc thinks, according to legend, this is the land of Porlock. This thrills him. He must be very near the Serpent River. The fading trail of deer prints takes him to the top of an escarpment. The captain catches his breath while surveying the vast valley beneath. A stream runs along the edge of the cliffs below. He traces it as far as he can. Then he sees it; the mouth of the Serpent. He's made it. He sits back against a stone, pulls an apple from his pack and takes a big bite, smiling, shaking his head. He has made it to the mighty Serpent.

While resting, Vandoc spots the same pack of wild skydeer running across the distant floor of the valley below, leaving a dust cloud in its wake. Genghis will soon set. The deer must to be headed to the river for an evening drink.

Then suddenly, across the vast valley floor, something can be seen moving, stirring inside the largest of the limestone caverns within the distant cliff wall. What emerges from the mouth of that cave cannot be encased in word. What emerges is an abomination of nature that should never have been; a beast unlike any ever known.

Frozen in fear, Vandoc observes from afar. This *Porlock,* for lack of better, stands upright on its hind two legs, reaching a height of what looks to be at least ten meters. Even from far away, it is repulsively difficult to look at. It has a bug-eyed exoskeleton, resembling an enormous insect. Its head is ant-like with what look to be antennae. Its body is that of a mantis, yet with the back legs of a reptile. Whatever the hell it is, it has obviously been genetically altered, and not according to galactic standards.

      "Holy sheep shit," Vandoc whispers to himself, crouching to avoid being seen. "A myth my ass," he adds, referring to standard belief taught within Colonial Intelligence that Porlock was invented by the Kingdom to keep the Pawani away from Mythos.

This mighty Porlock suddenly spots the deer, which have stopped dead in their tracks to avoid detection. The beast crouches back down on all legs, then leaps forward in pursuit of the pack. The deer immediately spring into a sprint for the treeline of an ancient orchard of dead trees that lie on the edge of the plain, just before the Serpent River. Upon the cliff wall, the captain remains frozen, watching two dust clouds move across the vast basin, one gaining on the other at unfathomable speeds.

"Come on," the captain says under his breath, clenching his fists. "Get to the trees. At least there you have a chance."

The deer do make the orchard seconds before the beast, then flee in different directions. The Porlock lunges headlong into the trees in pursuit, shredding limbs. Its head remains visible above the treeline, moving into what appears to be an attack mode. A patch a trees rustle and a cloud of dust rises. Soon, the Porlock emerges from the orchard with two deer; one in each clutch, destined to suffer the grizzliest of fates. One of the two remains conscious. The Porlock slams it down on the ground and drops down on it with a knee to crush its legs. It does so to immobilize the poor creature, yet keep it alive and thus fresh. The crippled deer is then forced to watch the Porlock rip a leg from its unfortunate pack-mate and proceed to devour it.

From afar, Captain Vandoc watches in sheer shock. Then suddenly, the beast stops feasting on the deer. It turns its head to look in Vandoc's direction. A chill runs down the captain's spine as he ever-so-slowly crouches deeper to avoid the Porlock's gaze. The beast, however, does not stop staring straight in his direction.

"Take a deep breath," the captain tells himself. "He can't possibly see you here."

Vandoc waits motionlessly, but the eyes of the beast remain locked. For a second, the Porlock looks away. The captain sighs. The beast then, however, takes its first step away from its fresh kill, in the direction of the escarpment. The captain freezes. The Porlock slowly takes another step, crouching. Vandoc lowers his head further. The beast suddenly breaks into a full sprint toward the escarpment, leaving a trail of dust behind.

"Oh fuck," the captain yells as he lowers himself below the rocks, out of view of the charging beast. "He's coming." Vandoc takes off running, down into a rock ravine. He hears a horrific shriek in the distance, getting louder.

An estranged skydeer passes him, also running for its life. The captain follows it into a cave on the cliff's wall, dropping to his knees and rolling to get through its entrance. The skydeer cowers as the calls of the beast grow louder, quivering behind a stone as the captain stands quietly against the cave's inner wall. The shrieks grow piercingly loud, then stop. The captain and the deer sit in pure silence, breathing deeply and slowly.

The sound of stone can be heard, sliding across stone. It occurs in short intervals. The frightened deer looks at the captain. The sound continues. With feline grace, the captain moves closer to the entrance to see what's going on. He quickly sticks his head out, sees nothing, and pulls it back. He hears the slide of a stone again, louder, closer to the entrance of the cave. He sticks his head out again, and this time finds himself staring straight into the ghastly face of the beast. The Porlock shrieks, then charges the cave. The captain jumps back just in time to avoid its pinchers as the beast slams head first into the cave, too large to get in. The captain backs up to a wall as the beast disappears. The sliding stone is heard again. There is silence, then again, the stone is heard. This time, a massive stone slides in front of the entrance, blocking access to the cave. The captain looks through a slight opening to see the bug eyes of the beast staring back at him.

"What the fuck?" Vandoc yells. Seconds later, he hears echoes of himself far, far away. "What the fuck?" again, and again. "What the fuck?" The Porlock's antennae perk up and point in the direction of the distant echoes. The beast runs off in that direction. The deer approaches the captain and rubs his head against his legs.

"He's clever," Vandoc tells the deer. "We're trapped in his pantry, on his shelf for dinner."

Using his flashlight, Vandoc discovers a small opening into a larger connected cavern. He combat-crawls his way through the opening. The deer follows closely behind. Neither of them look back, nor even want to know what lies beyond this cavern. They follow it further into the inside of the escarpment, through a porous membrane of caves, looking for safe passage. They arrive at an open-air enclosure, tucked well within high cliff walls, with no opening into the enclosure larger than a meter in diameter. They have found sanctuary, for there is no way for a three-story insect to get into this place. They stop to catch their breath, safe for the time being.

The high cliff walls provide a narrow but clear view of the darkening sky. Pyro lights up the night like a spotlight, illuminating the cliffs. The rest of the visible sky is endlessly speckled with stars. Vandoc and the deer rest beneath the twinkling sky, nestled within the protective walls of their new-found Shangri-La. Sheer fear fades to meaning as the shivering deer again lays its head to rest on Vandoc's thigh.

"We're alive," Vandoc tells the deer. "Did you hear that, Creed?" he says as he looks up at Pyro. "I'm right here you asshole. Oh, pardon me, asshat. I'm alive, Creed, and right here in front of your revolting face."

The captain then scans the stars for the dimmest among them.

"Did you hear that baby?" he asks with far less conviction in his tone, somewhat broken. "I'm alive. I'm still alive."

Chapter 21

"If he's alive, he'll find his way back to me," Nebula tells Agent Sandbrook as she stares into the dark Martian night.

"I like to see such faith," Sandbrook replies. "How do you stay so strong?" he asks.

"I believe in him," Nebula answers. "He knows a lot about the Kingdom. He knows locations of hidden planets. He even knows how to travel the galaxy without using hylo-travel."

"How so?" Agent Sandbrook asks in dismay.

"He has discovered the Pulsar Path," Nebula answers; "using some theory he formulated after reading Commadore Trebok's book."

"I've heard of the Pulsar Path," Sandbrook notes with genuine interest. "Your husband sounds like a fascinating guy," he tells her.

"That, he is," Nebula replies with a nostalgic smile.

"Thank you for your time and I wish you a good night," Agent Sandbrook says as he vanishes holographically, leaving Nebula alone on her balcony beneath the stars.

Chapter 22

Genghis' first light cracks the cliff walls, striking Vandoc's face. It's hot and getting hotter. The deer wakes nestled next to the captain, who hasn't slept. He remains at peace, nevertheless, always finding euphoria in the moment. Here he is, deeper than ever within lands about which he has only heard, read, or dreamt, living a reality that just hours ago he believed to be myth. If this is how he is to die, it has been quite a ride.

The deer attempts to stand but is weak and wobbly, growing more and more dehydrated by the hour. The captain pulls an apple from his pack and slices it into pieces to share with the deer.

"This will help, but we need to find water soon," Vandoc tells the deer. "We have to get the hell out of here."

The deer's strength soon returns and the two move on, out of the sweltering enclosure and into the cavernous labyrinth, looking for any possible way to escape the predator to which they've fallen prey. As they continue downward, they encounter beams of light entering the caves from the valley. An exit can't be far. They cautiously proceed.

They come upon a large cavern at the base of the escarpment. There are skeletal remains of several creatures in the cavern.

"We were led here," Vandoc tells the deer. "That grass-fucking-hopper steered us here like sheep."

Light shines through a long narrow gap. The captain draws carefully closer to the gap and looks through it at the vista. He can see the vast valley floor, now just a few meters below, the treeline, and the distant river.

"The Porlock doesn't cross the river," he says to himself, quoting Magnus. "Fire and water are its only known fears."

Suddenly, a massive hairy insect appendage sweeps into the gap, just missing the captain by microns as a piercing hiss is heard.

"Holy fuck!" the captain yells, as a massive black eye peers into the crack. His voice carries through the caves and into the valley, where it echoes, "holy fuck…holy fuck…holy fuck." Then it happens again; the beast backs away from the caves with its antennae now perked and pointed in the direction of the echoes. With little hesitation, the Porlock breaks into a sprint, chasing the echoes.

Exhausted and in fear, the captain crawls out of a wind-bored hole and onto a stone, where he surveys the valley. The deer remains inside the cave, still shaking from the encounter. Pyro lights up half the sky. The Porlock has vanished around a distant hill opposite the orchard and the river. The captain starts moving his right forearm back and forth in an effort to time the seconds of silence. A dry wind takes him by surprise, stirring up a momentary dirt devil. He stands there for approximately thirteen minutes before the beast reappears in the distance, returning from around the hill, again leaving a dust cloud in its wake as it races back. Vandoc crawls back through the hole, into the safety of the cavern. With the deer, he waits silently sitting against a wall just out of reach of the beast. Within seconds it is back at the cave, hissing and pissed after chasing empty echoes. Its black eye again peers through the gap and locks onto the captain like a laser.

"It's just over a 3K run to the treeline," Vandoc tells the deer. "I ran a 5K in 23 minutes in high school. Of course, I wasn't weighed down with a survival suit and I was decades younger. On the other hand, I wasn't running for my life," he says, weighing his chances. "If I wait a little while for his stinking fluid to refill, I can probably send him chasing another echo. I just need to make the treeline before being seen. From there, I can get to the river. If I don't make the treeline before being spotted, at least I don't die in this god forsaken cave."

Deep in thought, the captain strokes the deer's forehead.

"I shouldn't wait," he tells the deer. "It's hot and getting hotter. We have no water. I'm already feeling shaky at the knees. My adrenalin is flowing but will only for so long. This is it," he says, now realizing the caliber of his situation. One thing Vandoc has never been is indecisive. He may not always make the best decisions, but he knows when it's time to make them. His window is upon him. The beast hisses loudly again, wanting its lunch.

"Let his hunger be the weakness we exploit," Vandoc tells the deer. "You're welcome to run with me or use the diversion to escape, but I wouldn't stay in this cave," he adds. "He has brought us here for lunch." The deer looks at the captain as if to understand. The captain packs only the essentials he'll need, leaving a pack with cooking items in the cave. They sit patiently listening to the creepy cries of this massive insect, waiting for a lull in the gusty winds, for their moment to arrive.

Seconds go by, slowly, then comes the break for which they've waited. Suddenly, there is no wind to mask an echo. On instinct, the captain jumps to his feet and moves to the gap in the stone wall. With everything he's got, he hollers, "bite my ass!" The

Porlock makes a squealing sound and charges the rock opening, striking close to the captain. Then, it happens again; "bite my ass…bite my ass" can be heard bouncing off distant canyon walls. The beast pauses with antennae perked and pointed, then immediately dashes off in the direction of the echoes.

"This is it," Vandoc tells the deer. "We're on!"

The deer follows him through the hole, where they step onto the rock. They can see the beast far off, still running away from them.

"When he vanishes around that hill," the captain says, stretching; "we run like fuck." They watch the distant dust trail curve around the hill. "Here it comes; three, two, one, and let's go!"

With his eyes locked on the faraway treeline, the captain breaks into a moderate dash. The deer follows, pacing him. Seconds feel like minutes and minutes like days. The treeline suddenly looks not only further away, but like it's getting further yet with each stride. Vandoc's eyes remain locked on the trees just the same. They are his freedom, his hope. He can't bear to look behind him, knowing that any second, he could be torn apart limb by limb. If this is to happen, he doesn't want to see it coming. Forward he runs, now sweating but keeping a steady pace, trying to keep his breathing in rhythmic unison with his stride. Moments later, however, he begins to feel his muscles lose their oxygen. They will soon fail if he can't stop to catch his breath. A cascading flow of adrenaline down his spine, however, won't let him stop. He's either going to make the treeline, or collapse trying.

With his mouth now too dry to swallow and body now too dehydrated to produce more sweat, the captain finally reaches the treeline. The deer follows him into the deadwood orchard where he drops to his knees behind a tree, gasping for air. Delirious from his run, he sees the deer's head suddenly stick up. He sees something. The captain looks back to see a cloud of dust crossing the desert floor, headed directly at them. They've been spotted.

The deer disappears into the trees. The captain, aware that he now has no chance of making the river, pulls his laser fire-starter from his pocket and fires it at the tree in front of him. To his surprise, it immediately ignites. A gust of wind carries the raging flames to

the tree beside it. Making his way further into the dead forest, Vandoc continues lighting fires in his wake, building an actual firewall. The winds again come to his aid, lifting the flames high into the sky and spreading them not only limb to limb, but tree to tree.

Then he hears it; the oddest of outcries. As the fires rage higher, louder it grows. The captain then sees a sight beyond description; the flaming shape of the beast, engulfed in fire, squealing in agony. He pursues the captain, but in ever-slowing motion as fire consumes his exoskeleton. The Porlock now cries in agony as he burns alive. Free from fear or threat, the captain looks into the beast's dying eyes.

"It was never your fault," he says. "You simply acted upon your instincts. Travel well," he sympathetically whispers as the Porlock takes its last breath.

Out of nowhere, the deer reappears. They walk to the river together, where Vandoc fills his canteen while the deer drinks insatiably. Once refreshed, the captain strips from his sweat soaked suit and walks into the river in his underwear, laughing. The beast is dead. "I need a camera," he thinks; "nobody would believe this." After a soak and a little time in the sun to wring his clothes dry, Vandoc decides to walk all the way back to the cave to retrieve the pack he had jettisoned in order to make his run. He is still within his window of making Timeless Valley in the next two days. He decides to get his supplies, then be on his

The Legendary Escape of Captain Vandoc

way. He has no time to waste. He and the deer begin to backtrack across the sand, beneath a stunning view of Pyro.

"Ooohh damn," Vandoc says to the deer as he turns to see a massive fire burning out of control. "It's consumed the entire orchard, jumped into the ravine, and is taking out that entire mountainside. Oops!"

Chapter 23

"It looks like a volcano," Boron says staring up at Mythos from Creed's terrace.

"Mythos isn't volcanic," Creed replies. "It can't be a cloud either. It's directional and seems to be emanating from a point along the coastline, somewhere near the Serpent River. It's a fire."

"A fire!" Boron says. "Is that even possible?" he asks.

"No," Creed replies; "it isn't. Mythos has no lightning. There hasn't been a fire on the planet since the Pawani relocation."

"Could an incendiary object have found its way into Mythos during Unibon?" Boron asks. "Dyvok was raging pretty close to the point of exchange."

"Highly unlikely," Creed answers. "Unibon was over a week ago. It wouldn't take eight days for a combustible to drift to the ground and start a fire."

"You don't think Captain Vandoc could have anything to do with this, do you?" Boron asks.

In silence, Creed takes an extended look at billowing smoke.

"Prepare my ship for departure," he instructs Boron. "Set course for that fire's point of origin. We leave immediately."

Chapter 24

"Thanks for walking all the way back here with me," Vandoc tells the deer as they finally reach the flat stone outside the cave from which they began their sprint. "I'm tired. Can you believe we made that run? Funny what you'll do when your life is on the line."

Just then, a white light appears high in the sky. Something is entering the atmosphere. It slows, then changes course to align with the canyon.

"That's no meteor," Vandoc tells the deer. "It's a ship. Quick, let's get in the cave before it scans the valley." Vandoc crawls back through the opening and into the cavern, followed by his new four-legged friend. He gets a good look at the vessel as it glides by on a low approach through the canyon.

"Are you goddamned kidding me?" the captain yells, recognizing Creed's ship. "How did he find me?" he asks himself. Then it occurs to him; the fire. There are no fires on this planet. "He knows I started it," Vandoc tells the deer. "Just lay low. They won't find us in here."

The wingtips of Creed's mighty ship leave contrails as it glides into the canyon, slowing to a horizontal stop, then stirring a sand cloud all around it as it touches down beside the smoldering carcass of the Porlock. A ramp descends. Soon, Boron and Creed walk down the ramp. Stepping onto the blackened floor of the orchard, they look around to survey the valley.

"What the fuck was that?" Boron asks Creed as they stare at the charred remains of the beast.

"A bioweapon remnant from the war," Creed answers. "There were rumors something was out here."

"You're telling me that thing has been here for decades," Boron notes; "Damn!"

The ship signals a life form in the vicinity as the deer steps out of the cave.

"Get back in here," Vandoc tells the animal, but the deer stands frozen, looking out over the valley floor at the ship.

"What is it?" Creed asks Boron.

"It looks like a skydeer on the slope in the distance," Boron answers as he peers through the scope of his rifle at the deer.

"That must be what the beast fed on," Creed replies.

"So, what caused the fire?" Boron asks. "That thing wasn't fire breathing, was it?"

"No, it wasn't fire breathing," Creed replies. "Something went down here. Anyway, let's get out of here in case there is another one of those around," he adds, staring at the dead Porlock.

Boron aims his rifle again at the deer and fires, immediately severing the deer's hind legs at their thighs. It bellows in pain as blood gushes from its legs.

"I got it," Boron yells with a smile.

"Why the fuck did you do that?" Creed asks, pissed off.

"What do you mean?" Boron responds. "Those things were nothing but food for this beast anyway."

"Idiots like you will be the fall of the Kingdom," Creed tells him. "That deer had a fuck of a lot more purpose than you do. You are a moron. Do that again and I will shoot you."

"No," the captain says, gritting his teeth. Tears form in is eyes as he is forced to stay at bay, out of the ship's eye. "I'll be right there," he says to the panting deer as it tries to drag itself across the stone surface with only its two front legs.

Creed and Boron board the ship. Within seconds, it fires up, lifts to a hover, then begins to glide through the canyon. Vandoc stays low as it passes by before ascending into the sky. The captain springs to the deer's side. He cries at the site, causing tears to stream from the deer's eyes as well. The captain sits next to the animal. The deer looks him in the eye, lays his head on his lap, and dies.

"I'll kill you, Creed, if the chance arises," the captain says shaking his head as he puts a stone on a pile marking the deer's final resting spot. "I won't hesitate." Vandoc bows for a moment to think of his friend. Then to nobody, he speaks.

"Our friendship was forged through circumstance; comrades ensnarled by a great beast, as feed for that beast. Together we overcame that beast, only for you to be brought down in a senseless act of violence by a sociopathic asshat with a gun. Rest in peace, my friend."

With that, the captain grabs his pack and makes his way back to the river. He inflates his suit and swims all the way across; the entire span of its breadth. The current sends him further toward the sea. He eventually reaches the sanctuary of its southern bank, climbs out and dries in the hot sun. Once rested, he begins his journey inland, upriver to Timeless Valley.

Chapter 25

"Bring his pig-shit eating cellmate to my chambers," Creed instructs Boron; "and hook him up to the detector."

"What do you hope to learn from him?" Boron asks.

"Anything," Creed replies. "If that piss roach escaped, his roommate must know something."

Within minutes, Magnus sits at a small table in a dark room, connected to a machine. Unable to mask his fear, he shifts perpetually in his chair, trying to find comfort.

"Why am I here?" he asks a guard. The guard does not answer.

"You can relax," Creed answers as he enters the room. "You were brought here as part of a routine investigation into your cellmate's suicide."

"But I already answered your questions," Magnus replies. "Why the detector?"

"Captain Vandoc worked within my personal chambers," Creed answers. "We take further steps before closing the books on such matters." He signals for the assistant to turn the machine on. "Let me remind you before we begin," Creed adds; "lies are not tolerated within the Kingdom. They are punishable by death. If you simply answer all questions honestly, you have nothing to fear."

Magnus swallows dryly.

"Could I get a glass of water?" he asks. Creed gives the okay to a guard, who soon brings him one. Magnus drinks the entire glass in front of them. "Thank you, I appreciate it," he tells them. Green lights glow on the machine as he says it, indicating complete honesty.

"You say Captain Vandoc mentioned Mt. Dyvok specifically to you," Creed says.

"Yes," Magnus answers; "I believe his exact words were, 'Dyvok is calling me'." The lights on the machine continue to glow green.

"Did he tell you anything else regarding his plan to take his own life?' Boron asks.

"Nothing that I can recall," Magnus answers. The lights continue to glow green.

"Were you aware that Unibon was approaching?" Creed asks.

"Yes," Magnus answers.

"How did you know?" Boron asks.

"Vandoc told me," Magnus answers.

"How did he know?" Creed asks.

"He got the information from the onboard navigation systems on your ship," Magnus answers.

"This is a violation," Creed says. "Why didn't you report it?"

"I saw no reason to believe the information hadn't simply been accessed inadvertently," Magnus answers. "I didn't see any intentional wrongdoing." The lights continue to glow green.

"How familiar was Captain Vandoc with Unibon?" Creed asks.

"Quite!" Magnus responds. "He asked a lot of questions about Unibon, the Pawani people, our ways, and our history."

"About Mythos?" Creed asks.

"Sure, about Mythos as well," Magnus answers.

"One more question," Creed tells Magnus. "Do you wish that I were dead?"

Magnus takes a deep breath as pressure builds within him.

"Yes," he answers looking at the table. The lights remain green.

"Thank you for your honesty. You are free to go," Creed tells Magnus. Fear fades to relief on his face as he disconnects himself from the machine and quickly leaves the room.

"He may already know too much," Boron suggests to Creed.

"Oh, shut the fuck up," Creed replies. "I want forensic scans done on my ship's equipment. I want to see everything he accessed leading up to Unibon, anything he touched."

Chapter 26

Though weary, Vandoc moves swiftly along the winding banks of the Serpent, wasting no time. Life along the river proves more abundant than rumored. More deer are spotted along the way, birds are both seen and heard, and fish periodically jump in the river. The vegetation becomes a unique amalgam of native growth and earth-based plants and trees, themselves further remnants of Pawani pioneers. Fruit trees are endlessly abundant, producing fruits of all shapes, sizes, and colors, both known and unknown.

The captain follows the ancient Pioneer Way, still easily visible though last trodden over a millennia ago. How fascinating this would be to the Pawani, who no longer even have access to this planet.

"I can't even take a picture," he says to himself as he crosses an ancient footbridge. "I don't have a camera. Hell, I don't even know what day it is."

The captain walks all day and well into the night under Pyro's moonlight, along the ancient trail, over dunes, through meadows, a forest, to the top of a high mountain pass. Genghis cracks the mountain peaks just as Vandoc catches his first glimpse of what lies beyond; Timeless Valley, even dreamier than imagined. Though overgrown beyond recognition in places, the ancient trail still clearly marks the way into this now forbidden land. Vandoc proceeds down the winding scenic trail, beneath a waterfall and into the lush valley.

Morning light brightens as he walks beyond rolling fields of wheat, corn, even quasar root, all suckling from the Serpent. The further into the valley, the more the echoes of ancient Pawani culture crossfade into modern agricultural structures. The few ancient structures that survive this planet's industrial age would bring a tear to any Pawani eye, for what

The Legendary Escape of Captain Vandoc

remains are internment camps left over from the enslavement era.

Vandoc remains very aware of time, and it is ticking. His arrival is not a day too soon. This is the morning of his planned departure from this planet. He now just needs to find Central Port, which should be along the river, then get to Bay 6.

Chapter 27

Creed sits on his throne, drinking from a goblet, watching two topless women dance playfully in front of him. It is obvious by the looks on their faces, they've been ordered to do so. Boron enters the room.

"Why do you disturb me?" Creed asks.

"I have further news regarding the captain," Boron replies.

"Oh, what now?" Creed asks. "The guy is in the volcano for God's sake."

"Do you recall authorizing a live animal shipment on the eve of Unibon?" Boron asks Creed.

"What are you talking about?" Creed asks.

"On the eve of Unibon, you authorized and reserved a private live animal container from Mythos to Shangdu," Boron says. "Do you recall doing so?"

"That son of a bitch!" Creed replies.

"He had access to the ordering manifests?" Boron asks.

"Have we missed the shipment?" Creed asks.

"I can call ahead," Boron says.

"No," Creed responds; "we should handle this ourselves."

"We'll never make the scheduled departure," Boron says; "but it's reserved on a barge. We could easily beat it to Shangdu and meet it upon arrival."

"Ready my ship," Creed commands. "Tell the pilot to plot a course for Shangdu."

Chapter 28

Automation in motion surrounds the captain as he follows the riverbank into the Industrialized Zone. A few cameras are around, but not a soul. A long set of connected river barges float by, heading upriver, stacked with containers. The last barge is flat with fencing around its perimeter enclosing a herd of massive babe oxen,[3] packed ass-to-face, confined within the ghastliest of circumstances. The vessel slows and sounds its docking horn as it rounds the bend just ahead.

"It has to be near," Vandoc says to himself half out of breath. "The barges," he deduces; "must be headed for Central Port. There's only one flight out a day." He picks up his pace, exhausted but excited. "I can't believe I'm here."

Upon rounding the bend, the captain is suddenly staggered by the sight of an enormous platform in the distance, along the river's edge. Atop the platform sits a huge shipping module.[4]

"It's loading," Vandoc says as he breaks into a jog.

After an arduous struggle to cross a stench ridden marsh, the captain arrives at Central Port's main platform. He watches the oxen being mechanically driven from their river barge, forced to wade through river water onto a ramp that leads into the facilities. Vandoc spots a metallic ladder connected to the side of the building. It leads to a small platform with a door

---

[3] **Babe Oxen**: genetically modified oxen bred from ancient Chianina Ox DNA for meat production, a practice is outlawed within the Colonies. The name "Babe" is derived from the ancient tale of Paul Bunyan.
[4] **Shipping Module**: incredibly enormous shipping barge which itself connects in orbit to others like it to form supermassive interplanetary shipping barges.

leading into the building. There appears to be a keypad outside the door.

"This is it," Vandoc says excitedly.

He has to wrestle with overgrown vegetation. Obviously, nobody has used the entrance in some time. He reaches the ladder and climbs it to the platform. He presses LF-36Q175 on the keypad, a code he has been repeating in his head for days.

"Here goes nothing," he says as he hits enter, knowing everything is riding on it. A beep is heard and a red light illuminates. "You must be kidding me," the captain yells. He carefully types the code in again, LF-36Q175. Again, a beep is heard and a red light illuminates. He tries again. This time, the code not only fails but trips an alarm. A red light flashes and a loud sound can be heard all around. The captain climbs down the ladder, drops into the marsh, and makes his way across the water, laying low within the willows.

"Damnit," he shouts under his breath once across the water. The alarm can still be heard, but soon stops. The captain waits impatiently, watching his plan come unravelled as the last of the oxen enter the port. A few minutes later the empty barges begin moving away from the river docks. A short alarm sounds as gates close. A loud rumble can be heard from the platform as the shipping module's large engines ignite. It slowly lifts from the platform, causing hurricane force winds beneath it. Vandoc covers his ears as the thundering ship lifts further and further into the sky. He watches it carry his hopes away.

Chapter 29

Meanwhile, at the Forwarding Command Office (FCO) on Shangdu, Lt. Lumina Lancer, receives a message from a monitoring agent. It reads, "Do you know this man?" and shows an image of Vandoc trying to access the facilities on Mythos.

"Who do we have here?" she asks herself as she looks over the image.

Before she can respond, another incoming message flashes. "Colonel Creed arriving," it reads.

"What does a colonel want?" Lumina types.

"He says he's here to pick up a shipment from Mythos," the message reads. Lumina watches his ship come to rest on a platform beneath her office window.

"I'll handle this," she types before closing her messages.

Genially, Lumina greets Creed and Boron.

"Gentlemen, how can I help you today?" she asks.

"We're here to pick up a shipment," Boron answers.

"I see, do you have the shipment access number?" she asks.

"Yes, it's LF-36Q175," Boron reads.

"That's a live freight shipment," Lumina replies. "It's arriving in twelve minutes at Bay 33. I can take you there now."

"We would appreciate that," Creed tells her, looking her over creepily.

They take a tram to Bay 33.

"Are you prepared to handle your freight?" Lumina asks. "It is live."

"We're ready," Creed says with a smile, touching his gun.

They arrive and wait patiently as the massive module descends, finally coming to rest on the platform. Lights turn green and doors open. Lumina takes Creed and Boron onto the ship. They find the pod reserved by Vandoc. Creed and Boron draw their guns, causing Lumina to step away. Creed enters LF-36Q175 on the pod's keypad and a door opens.

Creed and Boron burst into the pod. Lumina can hear them shout.

"Thought you were clever did you, piss roach," Creed yells. "Where is he?"

"There's no one here," Boron answers.

"I can fucking see that, idiot," Creed replies.

The men do a quick search of the pod but find nothing inside.

"Did your cargo get away?" Lumina asks. "Should we be concerned?"

"No," Creed replies. "We thought it might not be on board. We just wanted to make sure."

"I see," Lumina says.

"You haven't seen anything suspicious lately, have you?" Boron asks.

"Suspicious, no," Lumina answers. "Why?"

"We appreciate your cooperation," Creed tells her.

Creed and Boron lift off. Lumina retreats to her office and pulls up the message with Vandoc's picture. "What was the access code he tried to use?" she types.

"LF-36Q175" appears on her screen. She smiles and nods.

Chapter 30

Wind whistles through the willows at the break of dawn. Vandoc boils water over a small fire, watching Genghis crack between the very mountain pass through which he came. He fears the fire may draw attention but has no choice. He has only two water purification pills remaining. When he's out of those, he's out of water. They have to count. All in all, he couldn't ask for better fortune; his timing, the winds, they all seem divine. If it wasn't for that damn access code. His plan left no alternatives, and no margin for error. Now, he has just that; an error.

"So close," he says to himself, shaking his head. "The ship was right there. So goddamned close. I had the code for Christ's sake."

Then, a beam of light appears through a layer of morning clouds, then another. Suddenly, through the clouds emerges a behemoth shipping module, gracefully descending toward the port.

"This is it," Vandoc says as he watches the ship come to rest; "my only chance to get off this planet." He knows the port schedule. He was scheduled on the second to last daily barge out before the planetary departure window closes. It's likely the last known vehicle off this planet for weeks.

He studies the scene carefully. When the steam and vapor from the touchdown clear, perimeter lights shift from red to green. The ship looks to be in boarding mode. Vandoc decides to give it another shot. Why not?

He works his way through the willows, the marsh, and across the stream. Again, he climbs the metal ladder to the access platform. Tired and shivering, he types his code in again; LF-36Q175. A beep is heard and again a red light illuminates.

"Come on," Vandoc says as he bangs his fist against the wall. Again, he types in the code, and again he is rejected. "Fuck," he yells. He goes to type it in again but stops short of entering, not wanting to trip the alarm.

Just then, he hears the docking horn of a river barge as it makes its way around the bend. Vandoc climbs down from the platform and stands beside the river, watching the ship dock. He studies every action as the river barge is unloaded, looking for a way in. The process is swift, all done mechanically with seemingly no room for error. Then the captain sees the final river barge dock, loaded with enormous blue oxen just as it was the day before. Vandoc watches them wade through the river, onto the ramp leading into the port.

"Here's my chance," he says as he wades back into the river. He puts his helmet on before submerging into the water. He remerges within the confines of the herd's fenced boarding area, standing next to the herd of oxen. Next thing he knows, he's walking out of the river, up the ramp, in the middle of a herd of gigantic blue oxen. Before he knows it, he's inside the ship with the oxen. Once all the oxen have entered, the gates close, followed by the doors.

The entire floor elevates, lifting the herd to the boarding level. It stops and gates again open. Moving walls force the oxen, and the captain, onto a boarding ramp. With no other option, Vandoc keeps pace, eyes peeled for a way to break from the herd. The opportunity, however, never arises, forcing him to bed with the mighty blue beasts in the cattle pod. The oxen lie to rest on a soft rubber surface. The ship's outboard motors rumble. The ship lifts off. The captain smiles as he envisions the view from the windowless chamber.

Once aloft, Vandoc lies to rest amidst the enormous blue beasts.

"I'm safe here," the captain tells the cud chewing ox beside him. "They have to provide us with air, water, and likely food. What is our onboard meal?" he asks laughing. The ox looks at him and bellows out a deep "mmmooooo." The captain rolls over to find himself looking eye-to-ass with another ox. Its ass winks at him, giving off the sound of pressurized air from a valve. Seconds later, Vandoc's eyes water at the powerful pungency.

The Legendary Escape of Captain Vandoc

"For God's sake," he yells, fanning the air; "what did you eat?" Just then, another unleashing is heard, bringing more tears to the captain's eyes. He moves away from the oxen, into the corner of the container, where he spots a door with an illuminated keypad. He tries the handle but it's locked. Frustrated, he turns around, only to be hit with further flatulence. "Oh, for fuck's sake," he yells at the oxen as he gags; "how much ass can you guys drop?"

What the captain doesn't know is that his attempt to open the door has tripped an alert back at FCO. A light blinks on Lumina's screen. "What now?" she asks as she accesses the video feed into the container. Immediately, she sees Vandoc with his back to the wall, literally. "Who do we have here?" she asks herself. Intrigued, she watches for several minutes. Finally, she accesses the ship's intercom and speaks.

"Undeclared interplanetary travel is strictly prohibited," Lumina's voice can be heard over the ship's com link. "Who are you," she asks; "and how did you get on board this ship?"

"I walked on with the oxen," Vandoc yells. Silence ensues. "Can you even hear me?" he yells.

"I can hear you," Lumina answers. "Mythos is forbidden. What were you doing there?"

"I'm Caribon," Vandoc answers to conceal his identity, causing Lumina to chuckle off mic.

"Well, Caribon, I have no choice but to report you," Lumina tells him. "There is no reason for you to sleep among the oxen, however." Looking at her screen, she tells him, "Enter code #6782970 to open the door. On the other side, you should find the ship's dockhand quarters. It's not much, but there is a washroom with a shower. There may also be some provisions. Help yourself. It's a long flight."

"I can never express my gratitude," the captain answers. "The methane in here is killing me."

"I can imagine," Lumina says, sympathetically.

"Why are you helping me?" Vandoc asks.

"I'm not," Lumina answers. "The quarters are something you could have stumbled upon on your own had you stayed to the far left when walking up the ramp with the oxen. As far as I know, that's what happened."

"In that case, I am truly grateful for your non help with what didn't happen," he replies. "Oh, what's that number again?" he asks.

"6782970," Lumina answers unsympathetically. She smiles momentarily with a twinkle in her eye as she watches Vandoc turn to give the oxen a final salute before leaving the herd.

Once through the door, as told, the captain finds living quarters equipped with a private toilet, shower, bed, and a kitchenette with fresh water and a cupboard full of canned foods. Vandoc immediately opens a can of stew and eats straight from the can. He has a tall glass of fresh water, then hops into the shower. Hot water has never felt so good. Once out, he lies on the foam bunk, out of his suit.

"What is to become of me?" he asks himself aloud. "Will they turn me over to the police or the military? Will I be executed? Sent back to Pyro? Both? Was there another way off this vessel?"

Chapter 31

Floating holographic documents surround Agent Sandbrook. Among them, the book *Beneath the Galactic Plane* - by Commadore Trebok. Three quick pongs alert him to an incoming message. It simply says "Microns" in its title. The agent hits play.

"Hello, Agent Sandbrook. Tyban, from Microns in New Kublai," the message begins. Sandbrook instantly recognizes Tyban. "You asked me to contact you if that guy ever came back. Well, he's here right now," he goes on to say as he lifts his fon to show the bar behind him. A man fitting the description of mystery man at the bar on the night of Vandoc's disappearance sits at the bar chatting with other patrons. "I'll see how much more I can find out," Tyban says. The message goes black, then immediately comes back on. Only this time, Tyban appears to be recording the transaction as the mystery man pays his tab. His face is clear and aligned in the image. "Sorry, that's the best I could do," Tyban adds just before the message ends.

Agent Sandbrook replies to Tyban's message with, "You did the Colonies a service. Thank you. Just a quick follow-up question," he adds; "how sure are you this is the same guy who was there on Christmas Eve?" He hits send, then opens mystery man's image through a facial recognition filter.

"I'll be damned if now we aren't getting somewhere," Sandbrook says smiling as "no match" blinks on his screen. "I'll be damned to hell."

Chapter 32

Vandoc steps onto his terrace to find Nebula leaning against its rail with her back to him.

"I told you I would be back," Vandoc tells her as she looks out over the canyon.

"I knew you would," Nebula replies, wind in her hair. "I have to tell you something."

"What is it?" Vandoc asks.

"I met someone," she says as she slowly turns to face him. The captain hears unpleasant, familiar laughter. He turns to see Creed walking out of his bathroom with only a towel around his waist.

"Captain Piss Roach," Creed says laughing.

"What the hell is he doing here?" Vandoc asks Nebula. She looks down. "What..."

Vandoc wakes to the sound of the module detaching from the greater barge. He abruptly sits up in fear. He hears Lumina's voice over the system.

"You will soon start your descent to Shangdu's surface," she says.

"Do you really have to turn me in?" Vandoc asks, not even sure if she can hear him.

"I could lose my job and possibly face criminal action for aiding a deserter," Lumina answers, clearly under the impression Vandoc is a member of Khan's military.

"I see," Vandoc replies, not wanting to correct her.

"What kind of suit is that?" Lumina asks.

"I'm a pilot," Vandoc answers. "It's a survival suit. I took it when I deserted, to survive."

"It looks military issued," Lumina replies.

"Look," Vandoc tells her, sensing her soft side; "they very well might execute me if they send me back."

"That seems a bit extreme for a runner," Lumina responds.

"I'm not a normal runner," Vandoc tells her. "I've seen things I shouldn't have."

"Someone came here yesterday to apprehend you," Lumina tells him; "to send you back to the military. His name was Creed."

Despair overtakes Vandoc's face. He sits on the bunk staring at the floor, expressionless. Lumina watches sympathetically.

"I don't want to know. It's better that way. I never saw you," she says.

"What?" Vandoc asks.

"I never saw you slip onto the ship and into the dockhand's quarters," she answers.

"Right, okay," Vandoc replies, confused.

"Neither did I see you slip off the ship after landing, nor did I give you any advice on how to do so, which in theory would be for one to follow the steps you took boarding, in reverse however. Once off the ship, one could part with the herd following the flow of the Orkhon River, turning right when it forks, away from the metropolis of New Shangdu. Within several hours' walk, one would find caves on the edge of the sea that offer refuge and shelter. Were one, theoretically of course, to follow the sands of that sea further northward, one would reach the village of Noradox. Therein lies a Pawani Temple. The

The Legendary Escape of Captain Vandoc

steward of this temple is known within the tightest of circles to assist deserters."

"Thank you," Vandoc says.

"For what?" Lumina adamantly inquires. "I said nothing; I saw nothing; and I know nothing," she adds.

"Got it," Vandoc responds smiling. "You don't hear this, but you may have just saved my life." Lumina smiles.

"Oh, and Caribon," she says; "one would also be wise to take whatever provisions one might need from the deckhand's quarters. They wouldn't be missed." Vandoc smiles.

Chapter 33

Kicked back in his zero-gravity recliner, Agent Sandbrook drifts between consciousness and sleep. He soon sinks into a deep snore, only to be woken seconds later by the repetitive pongs of an incoming message. He takes it. Tyban appears in front of him on a floating screen.

"Damn," he says; "that's how certain I am that it's the guy from Christmas Eve. Damn certain!"

Sandbrook smiles, then pulls up the images Tyban sent him. A repetitive scan of the face in the image occurs. "No match found in system" flashes after each of them.

Chapter 34

The captain stuffs a pack with canned food and a blanket from the dockhand's quarters as the gigantic vessel sets down. He fills his canteen, then waits. Soon the massive retro-rockets shut down and the bay doors open. The sky is dark. The oxen begin moving down the dock ramp toward another river barge which awaits them on the banks of Shangdu's mighty Orkhon River. Vandoc follows. Soon, he's able to give his herd the slip as he wades into the river, swim around a fence, and escape into the night.

As instructed, the captain follows the river downstream, unaware of the time, the day, or even really where he is. He's read of this planet, but so little of it. Now here he is, stranded on it, making his way through its darkness. Looking up, he laughs as he spots what appears to be a set of stars so far away, one slightly brighter than the other and giving off a bluish hue; Mythos and Pyro.

 "I'm way over here now, Creed," Vandoc yells at the night sky. "I made it."

Like all other populated celestial bodies in the system, barring Mythos, Shangdu has been terraformed. It was a good candidate and its terra-formation went well. Unlike Mythos, Shangdu is populated, largely civilized, and boasts of a low crime rate. It hosts a large Pawani population, mostly from the Great Relocation, when Pawani were forced to resettle from Mythos. Streets run along the Orkhon, but the captain avoids them, staying out of street light. This further impedes his trek, but with nowhere to be, time is now back on his side. Kilometer by kilometer, he makes his way along the river, beneath a blanket of stars, deeper into the night. For the first time in a long time, a sense of freedom tingles down his spine, no longer having to adhere to a do-or-die timeline. His hopes have been revitalized. Now, he just needs a plan.

Two of Shangdu's three moons rise above the valley. To think, their light originated in Genghis' core, then bounced off their surfaces before bouncing once again off the surface of this winding river, leaving just enough ambient light for Vandoc to follow its bank. The night sky fades from black to deep morning blue as the captain reaches the foretold fork in the river. He remains to its right. Aircraft lights cross the busying blue sky. Stars dim into day, one by one.

An hour or so beyond the fork, a moonlit ocean comes into view. The sight almost brings a tear to

Vandoc's eye as he takes in the beauty of this new planet. Moonbeams bounce off the ocean's calm surface. The air is fresh and the scene is dreamy. Along the ocean's edge, the captain finally reaches the caves. He takes shelter in the first one he can find that looks both private and safe. Inside, he sets up camp, builds a fire, and relaxes, staring out over the endless ocean.

Chapter 35

Meanwhile, at the Martian headquarters of Shorebok Shipping, Agent Sandbrook and Inspector Perry sit patiently in a conference room with a stunning view of Olympus Mons.

"I could just stare at that all day," Sandbrook says as he looks out of the big bay window.

"We have nothing," Perry tells Sandbrook. "What do you hope to gain here?" he asks.

"Something," Sandbrook answers; "I hope to gain something from nothing,"

"And how do you hope to accomplish that?" Perry asks.

"By doing nothing," Sandbrook answers.

"Nothing," Perry restates.

"Nothing," Sandbrook replies, still staring out of the window.

Into the room walks Nario. The three men exchange greetings, then take a seat around a glass table.

"So, what can I do for you gentlemen?" Nario asks Sandbrook and Perry. "Any new developments in the case?"

Agent Sandbrook doesn't answer verbally, but he cracks a confident smile upon hearing the question. Sandbrook and Perry look at each other as if to be concealing something. Finally, Sandbrook speaks.

"You mentioned talking to someone in Microns on Christmas Eve," he says; "on the night that Captain Vandoc disappeared.

"Yes," Nario replies. "If that's what I said. It has been a while."

"Indeed," Sandbrook responds. "Maybe this will help refresh your memory." He puts his fon on the table and taps it twice. A holographic image of Maxiums Krylok appears. Sandbrook goes back to staring out the window, saying nothing. Inspector Perry observes.

Time slows to a standstill. Finally, Nario breaks the silence.

"Yes, I remember bumping into him that night as well," he says. "In Microns."

"So, this is not the man you mentioned in your earlier report?" Sandbrook asks.

"I don't remember exactly what I told you guys, but no," Nario answers; "that was another guy I may have talked to in the lobby. I probably just confused the two."

"Do you know this man?" Sandbrook asks.

"Yes, he's my freight forwarding agent in New Kublai," Nario answers.

"What is his name?" Sandbrook asks.

"It's Ryk," Nario answers.

"Just Ryk?" Inspector Perry asks, breaking his silence.

"I don't remember his last name," Nario responds.

"I would imagine that you have Ryk's name and contact information on file," Sandbrook notes. "I don't suppose you would mind if we got in touch with him. We'd like to ask him a few questions."

"I'd love to help you, Mr. Sandbrook, but it's our company's policy not to share client contact information with anyone, including law enforcement unless under subpoena. I'll tell you what I can do, however. I can look Ryk up and contact him myself. I'll explain who you are and ask him to contact you directly, should he wish to assist you. That way I won't be breaking protocol. How does that sound?"

"Lovely," Sandbrook answers. "We'll be looking forward to hearing from him."

"Yes," Nario replies; "hopefully he gets back with you in a timely manner and can be of assistance to you."

"Yes," Sandbrook responds; "hopefully he does."

Chapter 36

Captain Vandoc sits on the beach beside a fire, smiling at the sky as he watches puffy pink clouds drift slowly over an unknown sea, into the horizon. It's mesmerizing. He takes a bite of chili out of an open can on the fire, then breaks into laughter, high on the moment. Sure, the odds remain against him, but he has been beating them. His wits alone, however, have not brought him this far. Fortune has smiled upon him; timing, circumstance, the winds. It's as if he's living out a legend. Could he be Caribon? And who is this mystery woman over the com to whom he owes his life? He wonders.

Lying low, Vandoc waits for night to drop before continuing onward. In the dark, he follows the coastline, eventually arriving at the seaside village of Noradox. The town is small and has but one central road. The captain follows it until he spots a building with ancient Pawani symbols aglow in neon signs within its windows. A marquis outside informs patrons of service times. A stairwell on the side of the building leads to what appears to be a basement bar. The sound of piano music over laughter carries from it. Vandoc follows it down.

Inside the bar, the captain finds a small but lively group, drinking libations and laughing. The music is not live, but soothing just the same. Vandoc approaches the bar.

"What can I get you?" a guy working behind the bar asks.

"I'm looking for the steward of the Pawani temple," Vandoc answers.

"I'll see if he's available," the bartender answers. "Now what would you like to drink?" he asks.

"I'm afraid I haven't the means to pay for a drink," Vandoc answers.

"Well then, this one is on the house," the bartender replies as he pours the captain a large glass of wine.

"Thank you, my friend," the captain replies. He then raises a glass to the bartender and takes a good sip. "Wine has never tasted better in my life," he tells the bartender.

"I am Forbin, the person you seek," the bartender tells Vandoc.

"You're the Pawani priest?" Vandoc asks.

"Yes, though Temple Steward would be my true title," Forbin replies; "and you are a ship pilot, running from something."

"Damn, how did you know that?" Vandoc asks in dismay.

"I was foretold of your arrival," Forbin answers.

"The mystery woman," Vandoc says; "of course. I'd like to thank her."

"Perhaps you'll get the chance sometime," Forbin says. "For now, the less people know, the better. Now, I don't mean to rush things, but I have a service to conduct. If you could grab your drink and follow me, I'll take you to where you can rest. I'm sure your journey has been long."

"To say the least," the captain replies.

Forbin guides Vandoc out of the bar and into the tower. Among inspirational posters on the wall in the tower lobby, Vandoc chuckles at one depicting the Porlock as a huge hairy creature. He is led up a spiral staircase to a small private room with a bed.

"Until we figure out how to introduce you," Forbin tells Vandoc; "let's keep you out of sight."

"Fair enough," Vandoc replies.

"There's a washroom with a shower in the hall. It locks for privacy. There is a small kitchen off to the right with some food in the fridge if you're hungry. You can check the donation bins for any clothes you may need. You should be alright here. If anyone asks, don't give them your name, which I've been told is 'Caribon'."

"Vandoc," actually, the captain answers; "Captain Vandoc."

"It's nice to meet you, Captain Vandoc," Forbin replies. "It is frowned upon within our faith to impersonate a prophet."

"My apologies," Vandoc tells Forbin. "It was the only alias I could think of at that moment."

"Good night, Captain," Forbin responds. "We're days away from our New Year, so I'm quite busy. I have to run. I'm off to conduct a service. Though I don't think you should mingle until we know how to introduce you properly, you are welcome to watch its telecast," he says, pointing to a floating holographic image.

"I can't thank you enough for all you are doing for me, Steward Forbin," Vandoc answers. "Please allow me to help you in any way that I can while I'm here," he adds. "I'll tune in to your service."

The captain takes a hot shower. The water feels better than any ever has. Once out, he finds some comfortable clothes from the donation bin, tucks his survival suit and pack under the bed, and lies down to watch the Pawani Temple services. He notices several of the people from the tavern. Then he sees, sitting alone, the most strikingly beautiful woman he's seen in a very long time. Vandoc can't keep his eyes off her as she sits with perfect posture, listening to Forbin welcome his congregation.

Once everyone is seated, Forbin starts his sermon.

"People have long wondered what the Porlock is," he begins. "Was it real or a metaphor? Was it an ape, a dinosaur, an alien? I wonder too," he adds; "but that's not what's important. What's important are the Porlocks we face in our personal lives every day, my people. Who is Caribon? We are all Caribon, I say. All men in every man…"

Again, Vandoc chuckles. He raises his wine glass in the air and takes a sip to mark the moment, then stares out a small tower window into the night.

"We are all Caribon," he utters to himself.

Chapter 37

A man lies prostrate in front of Creed's throne, nose pressed against the floor of the stone walkway. Creed's head begins to bob as he drifts to sleep. The servants about him exchange looks of dismay amongst themselves. One shakes his head while another shrugs his shoulders. Then Creed lets out a loud nasal snore, prompting Boron to signal for another soft strike on the chamber gong.

"What is your wish for the prisoner who lies before you regarding his theft of kitchen provisions?" the servant asks as he strikes the gong, well aware that Creed may need reminding of the charge the man faces. Creed awakens.

"Is this this man's first strike," Creed asks bitterly as he raises his head.

"It is," Boron answers.

"You will be issued a strike," Creed tells the prisoner, still lying face down. "Let it serve as a warning, because you will not get a second."

"You are most wise," the prisoner replies.

"Yes, I am," Creed replies. "Unfortunately, we don't keep a running list or database of strikes. Our system is a bit crude, but effective." Creed nods to a servant who then pulls a short rod out of a control panel. The end of the rod is shaped like a volcano and is aglow with heat. "This is going to sting, well, quite a bit," he tells the prisoner.

Guards hold him down. He screams in agony as the hot branding iron presses against the skin of his upper arm. "Now get him out of here," Creed instructs his guards. "I want everyone out of here."

The chamber clears, leaving only Boron with Creed.

"What if he missed the barge and is still on Mythos?" Boron asks Creed.

"Enough," Creed replies. "You heard his cellmate. He'd heard the call of Dyvok. One beacon doesn't trip and your mind wanders all over the place. He's dead. Leave it alone."

"One beacon, a helium lift, a fire on Mythos, and an unscheduled interplanetary shipment of live goods," Boron responds.

"All circumstantial for god's sake, let it go!" Creed yells. "He's in the volcano, where you'll be if you keep feeding this conspiracy. Now when I said that I wanted everyone out of here, I especially meant you. So, fuck along."

Chapter 38

A morning-show news desk appears in holographic video as Captain Vandoc crawls from beneath an elaborate lighting display. He's been working on it for the Shangdu New Year festivities. Dressed in casual Pawani attire, he blends well into the local scene.

"Welcome back to *Good Morning Kingdom*," a smartly dressed, handsome young host says.

"How surreal," the captain tells himself, mind-blown to actually be in the Kingdom, listening to Good Morning Kingdom, a propaganda show known throughout the galaxy.

"General Bontai is to be executed at dawn tomorrow morning for criminal concealment. The execution will be shown live on this channel," the host goes on to report.

Forbin enters the garaged area. Today, he is not alone. With him is a man and a woman; the same unforgettably attractive lady Vandoc saw attending Forbin's sermon. The captain's eyes widen, but he maintains as Forbin and the lady approach.

"Captain, I'd like you to meet your guardian angel," Forbin says pointing an open arm toward the woman; "Lumina."

"Yes, I recognize you from the security video," Lumina tells Vandoc with a warm smile.

"And I you from Steward Forbin's sermon the night after I arrived," Vandoc tells her. "I watched the cast." This makes Lumina smile widely, revealing more interest in the captain than she'd hoped to. They lock eyes for a second. "I can't thank you enough for saving my life," he adds.

"You're welcome," she replies.

"And this is Lumina's brother, Lok," Forbin says.

"A pleasure to meet you, Lok" Vandoc says.

"You guys are just in time for me to test the product of my morning's toil; a light display for the New Year's party." Vandoc hits a switch and the room goes dark. Soon, lights begin to twinkle like stars fading in and out.

"Oh my God, it's dazzling!" Lumina says with sheer excitement in her eyes. "Are you joining us for the celebration?" she asks Vandoc.

"I don't know..." Vandoc says.

"The captain still lacks an identity," Forbin reminds them.

"Captain," Lumina says; "if you don't mind, I'd like a quick word in private with Forbin and my brother."

"Not at all," Vandoc replies.

The three of them step into the corner of the room. The captain drifts toward the other corner to politely afford them their privacy, but continues to watch them out of the corner of his eye. Their discussion quickly grows heated before rapidly cooling. Lok shrugs his shoulders as if he doesn't care. Soon, Forbin follows, also falling into apparent agreement. They return.

"We have a way to help you," Forbin tells Vandoc. "We have an alias for you. If anyone asks, you can tell them your name is *Kyper*. You are Lumina and Lok's cousin, visiting from New Shangdu." Lok and Lumina look at each other in agreement. Unfortunately, that is all I can share with you at this time. For now, the less we say, the better," Forbin adds.

"Okay," Vandoc replies; "and know this; I will return the favor in any way I can, or die trying."

"We understand well what you're going through," Forbin tells Vandoc. "We are a nonviolent people who don't believe in involuntary military service.

"I have to tell you something about who I am," Vandoc says.

"Please don't," Lok says. "The less we know about you, the better. Penalties can be harsh for aiding deserters."

"I'll come by tomorrow afternoon with something you can wear to the festival," Lumina tells Vandoc.

"That's very generous," the captain replies. "Thank you all, deeply."

Chapter 39

Agent Sandbrook and Inspector Perry sit at a small bistro table on a mezzanine within the atrium of an enormous office building on Mars, chatting over coffee. Sandbrook is alerted to an incoming call; it's Nebula.

"What does she want?" Inspector Perry asks Agent Sandbrook.

"She probably just wants to be updated on her husband's case," Agent Sandbrook answers.

Agent Sandbrook takes the call, putting her on speaker.

"How are you, Nebula?" he asks.

"I'm fine," Nebula answers.

"I'm sitting now with Inspector Perry," the agent tells her. "We were actually just discussing your case. Would you mind if he joined our conversation?"

"Not at all," Nebula answers. "Have you learned anything new?" she asks.

"We have," Sandbrook answers. "Does the name Ryk Nybot mean anything to you?" he asks.

"No, should it?" Nebula replies.

"He was the third guy at the bar with your husband and Nario Shorebok the night Captain Vandoc disappeared," Sandbrook replies.

"I don't think my husband knows anyone by that name, and I don't know who Nario associates with," Nebula replies. "Have you spoken to the guy?" she asks.

"Not yet," Sandbrook answers. "We're waiting for him to get in touch with us."

"Is waiting for a suspect to call you standard protocol?" Nebula asks.

"No," Sandbrook answers; "but there are times when how someone responds tells us more than what they actually say."

"Let's just say it would be within Ryk's best interest to contact us," Inspector Perry adds.

"How much did Nario know of your husband's military service?" Agent Sandbrook asks Nebula.

"Hardly anything," Nebula answers. "He knew Vandoc had served, but nothing of the war or anything proprietary."

"If your husband was kidnaped for his military expertise," Perry asks; "how do you think the Kingdom would have learned of his high-ranking value?"

"If he was kidnapped by the Khan that is," Nebula replies. "Be that even so, who knows how they would know? They have countless methods and keep endless records. My husband knew the risks but took his chances. Something he did for us," she adds.

The Legendary Escape of Captain Vandoc

"Why did he feel the need to take such risks?" Agent Sandbrook asks.

"We've been having some money issues," Nebula responds. "Jonathan has made a few poor investments over the past few years. I think he may have felt compelled to make up for them. That's what I think drove him to take a risky job. He did it for us."

"We appreciate your insight," Agent Sandbrook responds.

"I want to find my husband," Nebula says. "I'm happy to provide any help that I can."

"Thank you," Sandbrook replies. "One more thing," he adds; "did Captain Vandoc tell you how he had discovered the Pulsar Path?" he asks.

"Vaguely," Nebula answers. "He said that his security clearance was necessary to connect all the dots."

"Fascinating," Agent Sandbrook says as his head slowly bobbles.

Nebula excuses herself and leaves the call.

"What is the Pulsar Path?" Inspector Perry asks Agent Sandbrook.

"It's a path of escape from the outer Perseus Arm, or the Kingdom, using the gravitational assist of an uncharted black hole to accelerate to hyperlight speeds fast enough for a ship to reach the Sagittarius Arm without the aid of hylo technology," Sandbrook answers. "The black hole is known in local legend as Notorbok."

"Is that so?" Inspector Perry says as he nods his head in thought. "Could Captain Vandoc have discovered it?" Perry asks.

"Why not?" Sandbrook asks. "His wife seems to believe he has."

Chapter 40

Two moons fill a darkening night that falls on Noradox. Distant drums echo from the shores of the Orkhon, beckoning locals from the village, down a path reminiscent of the ancient Pioneer Way, leading into a night of festivities. The year now has but a few hours remaining.

Clad in traditional Pawani festival wear, the captain takes one last look into his mirror before stepping out into the deepening night. The drums lead him down a torch-lit footpath through a grove of towering trees. Intensity grows with every echoing beat as the path draws nearer to the river's edge.

Diffused moonlight flows over distant cliff walls. Thick steam rises from springs, adding depth to the night.

Glowing rays from the torchlit path dance between silhouetted bamboo trees. The scene is mesmeric, forcing the captain to pause for a moment. The moment begats a conclusion; for whatever the risks, he has already experienced a five-fold return on his journey. For all the tales he's ever known, he is now living one of his own. The question now is, will he ever return to tell it?

Laughter fills the night as Vandoc comes upon a group of women giggling in the forest, excitedly helping one another change into Pawani festival

gowns. Then, through the deep mist, he spots her; Lumina. She's standing alone, staring up at the moon, wearing a thin, revealing costume that accentuates a certain curvature to her hips the captain hadn't noticed before. Entranced, Vandoc cannot avert his gaze, seeing nothing but her; the object in infinity.

The moment draws the attention of one of Lumina's giggling girlfriends, who notices the captain's interest in Lumina. She approaches Lumina, taps her on the shoulder and whispers something into her ear. Lumina looks over her shoulder to catch Vandoc's gaze. She smiles warmly, then gently slithers into her festival gown as the captain walks closer.

"You clean up well," she says as she looks over the captain's traditional get up. "Pawani looks good on you," she adds with a smile.

"You look fabulous," Vandoc tells her. They lock eyes for a second before Lumina looks away, still smiling.

"Come with me," she says as she grabs him by the arm. I can show you around.

"Thank you," Vandoc replies; "I'd really like that."

The night sinks into dream as Lumina leads the captain through the misty forest. Her gown allures, as it is designed to do. Pawani New Year is traditionally celebrated as a fertility festival; a time for mating, and festive wear is aimed to attract a mate. Each moonlit step they take prods a primordial passion that has been swelling within both of them from the moment they met.

"What a night," he tells her. "I haven't felt like this for a very long time."

"What is it that you feel?" she asks.

"Safe," Vandoc answers; "a sense of belonging, of home. I have you to thank for that," he adds.

"You're welcome," Lumina replies with a flirtatious smile and a sparkle in her eye. "We have no love for military conscription," she tells him. "Pawani are a largely pacifist people, yet we have by far the largest portion of our population serving in the Khan's armed forces. This is not out of any love for the Kingdom," she adds. "We lack the resources and opportunity to evade military service."

Vandoc smiles as he feels himself fall a little further under the spell of this endlessly interesting woman; his savior. Lumina catches him eying her over as he can't ignore the curves of her body, glowing in the moonlight. The subtle sway of her hips awakens something so deep within this forest, deep within this galaxy, and deep within his soul.

"Were you able to see any Pawani ruins on Mythos?" Lumina asks.

"I've been down the Pioneer Trail," Vandoc answers. A lot of it remains intact to this day," he tells her; "villages, orchards, trodden trails, artifacts."

"That's fascinating. You're an intriguing man," Lumina tells him. "There are many things I wonder about you, but in good time."

"There are a few things I'd like to tell you…" Vandoc says.

Lumina presses one finger against her own lips and another against Vandoc's. "They're safer left alone for now." The two lock eyes for a moment before Lumina slips out of his personal space; out of his face.

"We have a plan for you," she says.

"What kind of plan?" Vandoc asks.

"A plan to set you free," Lumina answers; "but tonight isn't the time for detail," she says laughing as they round a rocky bend leading into the makeshift markets that line the riverbanks, bustling with food, games, prizes, music and spirits; "tonight is a night for celebration!" she yells over the heavy, rhythmic beat of a drum circle.

The night is spent in laughter, eating traditional foods, drinking spirits, taking in arts and crafts, and dancing with the villagers to traditional music. Vandoc has the night of his life. Lumina couldn't have had a more tickling task either than to show 'Kyper' around. Four moons shine through the darkness; two in the sky and their reflections off the placid surface of the Orkhon.

"I can't begin to tell you what this night means to me…" Vandoc begins to say.

"Ssshhh," Lumina responds, again pressing her finger against his lips. "It's time. Do you hear that?" she asks.

"I don't hear anything," Vandoc answers.

"That's right," Lumina responds. "The drums have stopped. It's time."

Lumina looks deeper into the captain's eyes. The sound of Cicada from the riverbank blends with chanting from the villagers as they count down the last ten seconds of the year. In the dark, Lumina draws closer to Vandoc, eyes still locked, looking for a New Year's kiss. As villagers chant *four*, *three*, *two*, *one*, Lumina gently presses her body against Vandoc's. Their arms naturally find a way around each other, quickly evolving from traditional touching to a sensual embrace. The two continue to look deeply into each other's eyes as their faces gravitate toward each other. Their lips touch just as fireworks explode over the river, echoing off the clouds. All of it, however, goes unnoticed by Vandoc and Lumina as they hold onto the moment, locked in a kiss.

After coming up briefly for air, Lumina draws close to the captain, hoping to follow up. Vandoc, however, pulls back, withdrawing himself from the exchange.

"What is it?" Lumina asks.

"I've never been more drawn to anybody in my life than I am to you tonight," Vandoc tells her; "but I have someone out there."

"I see," Lumina replies.

"I'm sorry," Vandoc says. "I wanted to tell you."

"You've been gone for some time," Lumina replies in a saddened tone; "and with the trouble you're in," she adds; "how can what you have ever be the same? How can you ever go back?"

"You're absolutely right," Vandoc tells her. "I don't know if I'll ever get back, or what to expect if I do. I just know the vows we've made. It's really the highest bond we share in this universe; our word. For now, at least, I am bound by my half of the bargain."

Lumina's disappointment fades to understanding as she pulls away from the captain's embrace. Oddly, she finds herself even more attracted to him than before. Silently, they both look over the mighty Orkhon into a speckled sky.

Chapter 41

Nebula lies naked on her bed, gazing at the moon and stars in the clear Martian sky.

"He's out there," she says. "I can feel him. He's finding his way back to me."

"How do you know?" Nario asks from the bathroom as he stares at himself in the mirror with only a bath towel around his waist.

"I don't," Nebula answers. "I have no idea if he's dead or alive," she adds. "I'm rehearsing for Sandbrook. He asks a lot of questions."

"It's his job," Nario replies, gazing at himself as he pats a little water on his temples to tame his hair. "Our plan is foolproof, so long as we simply stick to it."

"I didn't expect him to ask me all the private questions about Vandoc, like what he reads. I mean, who cares what he reads?"

"What did you tell him?" Nario asks.

"I told him about his obsession with the war, the Kingdom, and about some of his strange beliefs," Nebula replies.

"Like what?" Nario asks.

"Oh, how he thinks he's found the hidden planets of Kerobot, and coordinates to the legendary Pulsar Path," Nebula answers; "to name a few."

"So, he could theoretically find his way back?" Nario asks in surprise.

"Vandoc's an idiot," Nebula replies. "He couldn't find his ass with both hands. He sank our money into an overvalued condo, where we're stuck hearing the Canyon Express. Then the clown blew the lion's share of our retirement trying to make up for it in the futures market."

"So, he's not an investor," Nario replies. "Maybe he's more clever than you give him credit. What if he has discovered the Pulsar Path?"

"Agent Sandbrook seems to think it's possible," Nebula answers; "thanks to the sincerity in my performance," she adds with a smile.

"What if he's dead?" Nario asks, not wanting to reveal what he's heard.

"He can't be," Nebula insists. "That wasn't part of the deal. I'm not a murderer."

"Nobody said you were," Nario says as he approaches the bed. "I'm speaking hypothetically. Accidents have been known to happen."

"So long as it is out of my control," Nebula says as she sits up on the edge of the bed; "I'm not to blame," she concludes.

She tugs on Nario's towel, pulling him closer to the bed. Her arms wrap around his waist before sliding down his bare back. Her fingers wedge between towel and Nario's skin, and begin working it free. Moon beams fill the room as the towel gently drops to the floor.

Chapter 42

The Legendary Escape of Captain Vandoc

Vandoc can't get last night's kiss out of his mind as he sits at a terminal in the resource center at the Pawani temple. Good Morning Kingdom can be heard in the background, coming from the lounge.

"Thank you Leaf. Our lead story at this hour is rioting, violence, and looting that went down last night during New Year celebrations on Shangdu, most occurring in the city of New Shangdu. The mayor has vowed to find those responsible and …"

"Happy New Year, captain," Forbin says as he enters the room with Lumina and Lok. Vandoc and Lumina's eyes meet, locking again for a second before breaking away.

"Happy New Year to you," Vandoc replies.

"How did you enjoy the festivities?" Lok asks.

"I've never had a better time," Vandoc answers sincerely. Lumina grins.

"Captain, we appreciate your patience and know you must wonder how you got your new name. Lok and Lumina are here to tell you," Forbin says. "This is also where I must leave, for it is better I not learn of their intentions," he adds. "Now, if you'll excuse me." He quietly leaves the room.

"So, who am I now?" Vandoc asks Lok and Lumina. "Who is Kyper?"

"Kyper is our cousin," Lumina answers. "He was beaten to death a few weeks ago by police in New Shangdu, where he's from," she adds solemnly. "We were quite close."

"I'm sorry to hear it," Vandoc replies. "So how am I to masquerade as your cousin? Isn't he now out of the system?"

"No," Lok says, "Kyper is still in the system. He was severely beaten, but those who beat him don't know that he died from his injuries. Very few of us know."

"What about his body?" Vandoc asks. "What happened to it?"

"It has been preserved according to Pawani customs," Lumina answers. "Pawani wait for the new year to bury the dead. It's bad luck for us to enter paradise in the year that we die."

"So, he's soon to be buried then?" Vandoc asks.

"His wishes are to be cremated, but his wishes are not that simple," Lok says. "That's where you fit in," he adds.

"How so?" the captain asks.

"We believe we have the means for you to legally assume Kyper's identity," Lumina tells him. "It's what he would have wanted."

"This sounds risky," Vandoc replies.

"It is," Lok says; "but it's been done before and we know exactly how."

"Dare I ask how?" Vandoc asks.

"That's where it gets a little gory," Lumina says.

"Gory?" Vandoc asks.

"Kyper was never a fan of the Khan. He had always planned to escape, so long ago he gave us his personal account information and all pass codes to hold onto. He told us to use what we could when he was gone to maintain the illusion he was still around. His bio-data is up for renewal, a time when an identity can be stolen," Loc answers.

"Bio-data," Vandoc says. "Let me guess. You want me to use a corpse to somehow gain access to the system."

"A finger and an eye," Lumina replies.

"I'm going to walk into some licensing office with a severed finger and eye," Vandoc says in a mild state of shock.

"Into an automated booth," Loc answers. "There should be no human contact if everything goes as planned."

"So, I use the finger and eye to access the booth," Vandoc says, suddenly intrigued.

"Yes, along with an access code, there is a retinal scan and a fingerprint match on the exterior access pad. Once inside, you'll be printed and scanned again to update your bio-data," Loc says.

"Won't there be any cross-referencing the data for similarity?" Vandoc asks.

"The system was programmed with a flaw. The computer runs a comparison, but always checks out regardless of the degree of discrepancy between their entrance data and their new scans," Loc answers.

"How do you know this?" Vandoc asks.

"As we mentioned, this has been done before," Lumina answers.

"Yes," Loc adds. "The guy who programmed the flaw into the system did so to escape himself. We helped him."

"You got him a finger and an eye as well?" Vandoc asks.

"They were reunited with their owner and given a proper burial," Lumina says; "as will Kyper's be."

"People donate organs all the time. How is this really any different?" Loc asks.

"It creeps the living hell out of me," Vandoc says; "but do I really have an alternative?"

Chapter 43

The following morning, Lumina, Lok, and Vandoc sit silently as they glide toward New Shangdu on a highspeed maglev. The captain looks nervously out the train's window.

"Remember, if this doesn't work and you trip the outer alarm, turn and walk swiftly away, get to the river and follow it to the caves," Lok tells Vandoc.

"And if I trip the inner alarm?" Vandoc asks.

"Then you'll be out of luck," Lok answers; "but don't worry. If you're in, there's no reason for the inner alarm to trip."

"I just hope they haven't fixed the flaw in their system," Vandoc says.

"Here are the items you'll need to gain access," Lok says as he pulls a small insulated bag from his pocket and slides it to Vandoc. The captain takes a peek inside to see the severed finger and eye, each air sealed in plastic wrap. His eyes immediately water as he swallows to hold back a dry-heave, then looks out the window to ensure nobody notices him.

"Arriving at New Shangdu Port Station in five minutes," an automated voice announces.

"Don't worry," Lumina tells Vandoc. "It's going to work. We'll be waiting for you just down the street, at the Portside Cafe. Come in once you have finished and we'll have lunch. We'll celebrate your new citizenship."

"Arriving at Port Station," is heard over the speaker as the train starts slowing. Each moment is an eternity. They all look at one another as they wait for the doors of the train to open.

"To think," Vandoc says with a nervous chuckle, "I'll either be sitting in a restaurant in a few minutes enjoying a new life, or back on the run.

The doors open. Loc, Lumina, and Vandoc step off the train.

"Here's where we separate," Lumina tells Vandoc. "We'll see you soon at the Portside," she adds, giving his arm a little squeeze for good luck before turning to walk away.

Vandoc makes his way out of the station, down the busy street, in perfect synch with the plan. He soon arrives at the booth; an automated records and archives mini-station wherein people within the Kingdom can renew any government credential automatically. He stares at the building for a few seconds like a deer in headlights. There is nobody using it; nobody in line; nobody around. The situation couldn't be more optimal.

The captain snaps out of his stare and into action. There is no time to think, only act. He casually steps up to the door, takes a quick subtle look around and presses the keypad. It lights up. He types the name Kyper Corlox into the pad. When prompted, he types in his Kyper's subject number and passcode. A green-light flashes as a pleasant beep is heard. So far, so good.

The system then asks for the retinal scan. Vandoc slowly reaches into his side pocket and pulls the eye out as he moves his face closer to the camera to align. Just as instructed, after his eye lines up with the camera, he moves the severed eye into place, shaking as he tries to hold it in place. He takes a deep breath and presses his wrists against the panel to mitigate the severe shake of his hands. It works. Soon, a beep is again heard, prompting him to place his finger on the pad for print identification. The captain laughs, for now the hard part is over.

He puts his hand on the sensor, then confidently slides the dead finger into his index finger's stead, holding it in place beneath his finger. He waits. No green light flashes and no beep is heard. After what seems to be an eternity, a red light flashes and a less pleasant, quick buzzer sounds. The screen again prompts the captain to put his hand on the keypad. Less confidently, he does so, slides the finger into place, and waits. After several seconds, the red light flashes and a buzz is heard again. The screen once again prompts the captain to put his hand on the screen.

"Is there a problem?" he hears a voice behind him ask. He turns to find a uniformed police officer standing behind him.

"No," Vandoc answers, then swallows to clear his throat; "it's just being a little stubborn today."

"The finger scanner?" the officer asks.

"Yes," the captain answers.

"It does that sometimes," the officer tells Vandoc. "The pad probably just needs to be wiped clean. It picks up oils and what not."

"Thanks for the tip," Vandoc says, wanting with every fiber of his being for the officer to go away. He doesn't. He just stands there waiting to see if his advice was sound.

Vandoc smiles then turns around, takes a deep breath, and wipes the pad off with his sleeve in front of the officer. Just as he'd feared, the officer doesn't leave. The captain ponders just walking away, but knows that would raise suspicion. He turns his back again to the officer, carefully pulls the finger from his pocket, and presses his hand once again against the pad. He closes his eyes as he again slides the dead finger beneath his own. He opens them to find the system in motion, processing the scan. "I can run for the river," he thinks to himself, fearing a third and likely final red light. Suddenly, to his ever-so-pleasant surprise, a green light flashes twice, a beep is heard, and a door opens to the booth's interior. The captain turns to see the officer smiling proudly.

"I'll be damned," he tells the officer as he cracks a wide smile. "It worked."

The officer walks away as Vandoc enters the booth. The door closes behind him. Once inside, he again has to verify his passcode, then line up for a new retinal scan and fingerprint, this time using his own biodata. He waits as the system contrasts the new data with the original; the final test. Was there really a flaw in the system? If so, was it fixed? Again, the captain grows nervous as the system takes an eternity to verify the biodata. A bead of sweat slides down his brow. "How about a little ventilation in here, for the love of Christ," he says nervously.

A green light flashes, signifying a match. Lok and Lumina were right. It worked!

"Your records are up-to-date and compliant," the system tells him as the door opens. "You are good to go."

Vandoc steps onto the street a new man. He can feel his adrenal glands relaxing as his stress rapidly evaporates into the beautiful Shangdu sky. He stands in a moment of pure relief before making his way down the street, laughing all the way to the Portside. Upon arrival, he spots Lumina and Loc inside, sitting next to the window, eagerly scanning the street. Her face fades from fear into sheer delight when she sees Vandoc enter. Loc sighs.

"Hey cousins," Vandoc says smiling as he takes a seat at their table, where he finds a full glass of merlot waiting for him, aerating.

"You are alone, I take it," Lumina says. "I mean like no police have followed you here or anything?" she asks.

"Not to the best of my knowledge," Vandoc replies; "nor do I see any reason for them too. My day is going smoothly."

"I'm thrilled to hear it," Lumina replies. "Congratulations!" she says as they all raise a glass, trying to contain themselves.

"So, tell me a little more about Kyper," Vandoc says. "Who am I?"

"Don't worry about running into your past," Loc tells him. "Kyper was a bit of a rolling stone. He doesn't have deep roots on this planet. But if you really do want to know, he was deeply devoted to his causes."

"Which were?" Vandoc asks.

"He envisioned a Kingdom without a Khan," Lumina says.

"He was even planning to join the Shadow Fleet," Loc says, obviously a little loosened from the wine.

"There is no Shadow Fleet," Lumina says.

"There is," Loc replies; "and Kyper was going to join them on Kublai."

"What is the Shadow Fleet?" Vandoc asks.

"It's a colony of people that live within the Kingdom while completely evading its scope. They live in the shadows," Lumina says.

"How so?" Vandoc asks.

"They exploit weaknesses in the Khan's interplanetary tracking system which allow them to travel undetected while being obscured by larger, moving objects. This allows for anonymous travel within the Kingdom," Loc explains. "It's a counter-tracking program the fleet runs that calculates voids, or shadows in the scans.

"That is brilliant," Vandoc replies. "Of course, the Kingdom still uses central-point planetary scanners. So, as long as you're behind a larger object in motion in relation to its scanner, you're invisible. You truly remain in the objects' shadows."

"Kyper could tell you more. He was really into them," Loc says.

"You mentioned that he wanted to join them on Kublai," Vandoc notes. "Does this fleet really travel to Kublai?" he asks with high intrigue.

"They camp on Kublai between the double moons, on Mystina Island, right under the Khan's nose," Loc says in laughter.

"Don't listen to him," Lumina says. "Who knows how true any of this is?" she adds, with a gleam in her eye.

"It could be the wine," the captain thinks to himself as he ponders the possibility of giving up his quest to return to Mars and just disappear. After all, "I've regained my freedom," he thinks, "and the most beautiful woman in the galaxy is sitting right in front of me." Then he imagines Nebula standing alone on their deck, waiting for him to return.

"Can we have our cousin's remains back?" Loc asks Vandoc. "Lumina and I will return to New Shangdu tomorrow to reunite them with Kyper's body. The mortician is a personal friend of ours who has gone out on a limb for us by not reporting Kyper's death. The sooner he can cremate Kyper's remains, the better."

"Can he incinerate something for me?" Vandoc asks Loc.

"What?" Loc asks.

"The survival suit I was wearing when I arrived," the captain answers. "It is all that is left to connect me to my previous life."

"We'll take it with us," Lumina answers. "I'm sure he'll do it."

"Yes, it would be within his own best interests as well," Loc adds.

They polish off two bottles of Pinot before finally deciding to head back to the station; back to Noradox. With a heavy buzz on, they opt for a less direct route, taking them through an older Pawani section of the city. Turning a corner, they're suddenly alarmed by the piercing sound of a siren going off right in front of them. Red and blue lights flash on every corner as flood lights turn on, filling the streets with high intensity beams of light.

"Warning, remain where you are," an automated but intimidating voice says.

Then it dawns on the captain; it's a police beacon. The blue stuff was still in his blood and he has tripped a sensor.

"They got me," he tells Lumina and Loc.

"Freeze," they hear an officer yell; "stay right where you are." Vandoc recognizes him. It's the same police officer from the booth earlier. "Hands out," he tells them.

Vandoc, Loc, and Lumina all extend their hands. The officer quickly scans all of their hands for prints. A green-light flashes.

"All clear here," he radios in to his office. "Could be a false alarm."

Chapter 44

Creed lies on his massive bed as three nude women rub oil on his hairy back. An old Martian movie has him laughing to tears. The moment, however, is soon brought down by Boron, who overrides it with an urgent interruption.

"For the sake of fuck, Boron, what is it now?" Creed asks.

"You have an incoming call from High Command," Boron tells him; "from Commander Nerabo."

"What does he want?" Creed asks himself. "I'll take it in my office. Tell Nerabo I'm on my way."

Creed tells his maidens to leave as he frantically springs to his feet to get dressed, not wanting to keep a commander waiting. He throws on his military coat but doesn't bother with pants, remaining completely nude from the waist down. He dashes into his office and takes the call.

"Commander Nerabo," he says as he answers the call, checking to ensure he is visible only from the waist up.

"Creed," Nerabo begins with a dead serious look on his face; "would you mind explaining to me how a police beacon just went off in New Shangdu with a direct link-code to your institution?"

Creed turns pale. He takes a second to collect himself, then speaks.

"Oh, that must be one of my prisoners out on shore leave, enjoying a shopping spree," he answers. "Probably stepped out for a coffee," he adds.

"Real fuckin' funny, Creed," Nerabo replies without expression.

"C'mon Nerabo," Creed pleads; "how am I supposed to know why some location beacon tripped. This has happened before," he says.

"Not in a very long time," Nerabo tells him; "and never with such an accurate match to a camp," he adds.

"Commander, all my prisoners are accounted for," Creed responds. "Aside from that, I have no idea what to tell you."

"Just doing my job," Nerabo replies. "If we don't pay attention to alarms, why have them?" he asks rhetorically.

"Was anyone apprehended at the scene?" Creed asks.

"No," the commander replies. "A few locals in the vicinity were checked, but were cleared."

"Sounds like a malfunction," Creed says.

"It does," Nerabo replies. "Just the same, I'd better submit this for further review."

"Don't do that," Creed begs. "You know they'll come here and wreck this place, and all for nothing."

"Yes, but it keeps my nose clean," Nerabo replies.

"I've got a case of Kentucky bourbon I've been meaning to send your way on a supply transport," Creed suggests. "Just let this one go. It was a glitch and you know it."

"I'll be looking forward to receiving that bourbon on the next transport," commander Nerabo tells him. "Good day, Colonel."

The transmission ends, leaving Creed shocked in its wake. Weak at the knees, he leans back in his chair to think.

"That mother fuck," he says as he pounds on his knee with his fist.

Chapter 45

Shangdu's setting sun glares in gold off the surface of the Orkhon. Vandoc, Loc, and Lumina sit again on a speeding maglev as it glides along the river, back to Noradox. Loc taps the window twice, sending it into shade mode.

"You set off that alarm, didn't you?" Lumina asks Vandoc.

"Yes," he answers.

"When were you going to tell us that you were a criminal?" she asks angrily. "We trusted you."

"I'm not a criminal," Vandoc replies. "You can trust me. The less we say, the better, am I right?" Vandoc asks. "Wasn't that what you told me? I planned to tell you as soon as it was safe enough."

"What did you do?" Lumina asks.

"Absolutely nothing," Vandoc answers. "I was taken against my will."

"Taken?" Loc asks; "by whom?"

"I was abducted by your military," Vandoc answers.

"What do you mean?" Lumina asks.

"I'm not a subject of the Khan or the Kingdom," Vandoc answers. "I'm a pilot from the Colonies. I was taken from a rigged com-box in New Kublai."

"Are you kidding me?" Loc asks, trying to keep his cool on the train. "You realize that you have put our lives in serious jeopardy."

"We're now facing high treason charges if caught," Lumina angrily adds.

"Look, it was selfish of me in retrospect not to have told you all this. I will move on very soon. I can't thank you guys enough for all you have done. I'm deeply sorry to have put you in danger and I vow to spend my remaining days seeking ways to make it up to you. Remember, I was never processed through your courts. We've already checked out with the police and my case has no military association. I think we're safe."

"Just how do you plan to move on?" Lumina asks Vandoc. "You're wanted by the military."

"If I can get back to Kublai," Vandoc tells them; "to the Neutral Zone at Port Kublai while a Shorebok freighter is mooring. I know the access code to their ships. All I have to do is board the ship to be considered in intergalactically neutral territory. I could be taken into custody from there and given a trial."

"Just how the hell do you plan to make it to the Port of Kublai's neutral zone?" Lumina asks.

"That's where I thought you might be able to help me," Vandoc answers. "This is your area of expertise."

"I can't be connected to this," Lumina says. "Working against the Khan is one thing, but with the Khan's enemy is another altogether."

"I would never ask you to put yourself in danger," Vandoc tells her. "If, however, you think of a plan in which any connection to yourself would be completely severed, I'm all ears."

"He is clean with the police," Loc tells Lumina; "and the military would never want this exposed," he adds; "but you can be certain of one thing; the colonel who came looking for you at the port will be back."

Chapter 46

Clouds of dust swirl around the huge landing gears on Creed's ship as it sets down on the plains just outside of New Shangdu.

"Wouldn't it have been more convenient to dock in New Shangdu?" Boron asks as they step out of their ship, onto the ramp.

"We are not here seeking convenience," Creed answers with an agitated look on his face. "We're here to snub a piss roach, and to do so discreetly. You know, sometimes I wonder what I could have done with the energy I've expended explaining things to your chicken brain," he tells Boron.

They take cycles to a nearby train-port where they catch a train into New Shangdu, disembarking at New Shangdu Port Station. From there, they find their way to the police beacon that Vandoc tripped. They look around suspiciously as they both carefully pull location wands from their bags, setting their sensors to high.

"If anyone spots us, we could be screwed," Boron says.

"If captain piss roach ends up caught by anyone but us, we could be executed," Creed says. "Now you go that way, and I'll go this way. Meet me back here in an hour."

Chapter 47

"Arriving on Platform Nine, the Orkhon Corridor Shuttle," a soft voice announces as a maglev slowly glides to a stop at Shangdu's Riverside Station. Lok and Lumina stand anxiously by the doors, and are the first to disembark when they open. They move at an unnoticeably brisk pace across the platform, down the stairs, and out the exit. Minutes later, they stand just blocks away, in front of Peaceful Transitions Funeral Home. A sign in front says, "specializing in Pawani burial customs."

Little do Lok and Lumina know, though, that Boron, who stands just around the block, has a beeping location wand, tripped by a dried blood stain on Vandoc's survival suit. With excitement on his face, Boron follows the signal until it fades, at which point he reverses direction. He walks until the signal fades again, then moves in a third direction, attempting to triangulate the signal's source.

"I think I've got him," Boron radios to Creed. "My wand has picked something up."

"Is the signal one of ours?" Creed asks.

"Yes," Boron answers; "undeniably."

"Don't lose him," Creed yells. "I'll be right there."

Boron closes in on the signal's source, turning the corner just as Lok and Lumina enter the mortuary. Creed arrives within minutes.

"What have you got?" Creed asks.

"He's near," Boron says; "but I can't pinpoint where."

"I'll go this way," Creed says as he turns his wand on. "We've got him. We just have to figure out exactly where he is without disturbing anyone." They hastily continue their search.

Meanwhile, inside the mortuary.

"We have an unusual request," Loc asks Dr. Rakasho. "We would like this survival suit cremated as well. We'd like to leave no record of it."

"That can be managed," Rakasho replies without asking why. "Do you have the borrowed parts?" he asks as he looks over the suit draped over Loc's arm.

"Oh yes," Lumina replies as she pulls a small pouch from her bag and hands it to Rakasho.

He takes the eye and finger over to a casket, opens it, and gently places them inside.

"Would you please join me in prayer?" Dr. Rakasho asks. Lumina and Loc approach the casket. They close their eyes and speak in unison, reciting ancient text from the Book of Time.

Outside, Creed and Boron find themselves facing each other as they round opposite ends of the same street; the very street on which the mortuary sits mid-block.

"He has to be on this street," Creed says to Boron as they meet in the middle, directly across from the mortuary.

Inside, Loc and Lumina watch Kyper's casket slowly move down a conveyor belt, into dancing flames. Rakasho takes the suit from Loc and lays it into a cheaper, cardboard coffin. He places it on the belt, just behind Kyper's wicker coffin. All three watch as it follows gradually into the flames.

On the street, Creed and Boron watch smoke rise from the stack of the mortuary.

"Looks like someone's going up in smoke," Boron says laughing. Creed's face remains emotionless. Just then, the signals on both of their wands quickly fade, then disappear.

"We're losing him. Go that way," Creed tells Boron. "Don't let him get away." They scurry away in opposite directions.

Several minutes later, they both return empty handed, with no signal, nothing.

"We have to get back to Pyro," Creed says. "People will start to wonder if we don't show up for initiation."

Lok and Lumina walk out of the mortuary and down the steps. Lumina looks over her shoulder and sees Creed just before she rounds the corner and disappears down the street.

"It's him," she tells Loc as they walk away.

"Who?" Loc asks.

"The creepy colonel that came to my work looking for Vandoc," she answers.

Across the street.

"Where have I seen her?" Creed asks Boron.

"The woman who just walked out of the mortuary with that guy?" Boron asks. "I don't know. I didn't get a good look at her."

Chapter 48

An elevated train passes by Agent Sandbrook and Inspector Perry as they stand surveying a street corner in New Kublai. Sandbrook points to an alley and tells Perry, "That's the captain's last known location. Something went down here that night."

He takes an incoming call.

"Agent Sandbrook," he answers.

"Are you guys still in town?" Tyban's voice can be heard.

"We are but running short on time," Sandbrook replies.

"Well, you're in luck," Tyban tells him; "I told the bus boy I'd tip him if your guy shows up at Microns. He just called. He's there right now, in a blue suit jacket, talking to some guy at the bar."

"You've made our trip," Sandbrook says with a smile. "We're just down the street."

Agent Sandbrook and Inspector Perry waste no time getting to Microns. Once inside, they immediately spot Ryk Nybot having a drink at the bar, engaged in serious conversation with some guy in a suit to his left. Sandbrook and Perry approach the bar. Sandbrook takes an open seat at the bar next to Nybot as Perry grabs the next one over, leaving three empty ones before the end of the bar. Ryk looks a little annoyed by the two of them sitting so close to him but carries on with his private conversation.

"You wouldn't happen to be Ryk Nybot, would you?" Sandbrook asks during a lull in Nybot's conversation.

"Do I know you?" Nybot asks as he turns his head to see Sandbrook and Perry.

"No," Sandbrook answers. Perry just watches.

"Who are you?" Nybot asks.

"My name is Sandbrook and this is Inspector Perry. We're in town to investigate the disappearance of a very important person," Sandbrook tells him.

"You don't say," Nybot responds. "So how do you know who I am?" he asks.

"You were one of the last few people to talk with him, the VIP if you will, on the night that he disappeared," Inspector Perry tells him; "from right here in Microns."

"Does this have to do with the missing pilot from Shorebok Shipping?" Ryk asks. "Nario Shorebok told me about him. I remember meeting him last Christmas Eve I believe. Nice guy. What a strange story," he adds.

"Yes, strange indeed," Agent Sandbrook says.

"Are you guys the ones that Nario asked me to contact?" Ryk asks.

"We are," Inspector Perry answers.

"I've been meaning to," Ryk replies. "I've just been so busy and truthfully, I'm not sure I can offer any useful information."

"What did you discuss with the pilot; Captain Vandoc?" Sandbrook asks him.

"I don't recall," Ryk replies. "Our conversation was brief. Oh yes, he told me about a condo he bought on Mars. That it was losing value, but he thought it would turn around sooner or later."

"Anything else?"

"No, not that I remember," Ryk replies. "I took off shortly thereafter."

"Where did you go from there?" Sandbrook asks.

"Why?" Ryk asks in return. "Look, I'm kind of in the middle of something here."

"We've traveled from Mars," Inspector Perry adds to the conversation.

"You don't think I had anything to do with his disappearance, do you?" Ryk asks.

"We don't think anything quite yet," Inspector Perry tells him.

"By 'quite' I take it you have some promising leads," Ryk suggests.

"We wouldn't have traveled all the way out here if we didn't," Sandbrook responds.

"Well, I sincerely hope you find the pilot, but I've just told you everything I really know," Ryk tells them.

"What is that?" Sandbrook asks as he sniffs the air.

"What is what?" Ryk asks.

"Can you smell that?" Sandbrook asks.

"Smell what?" Ryk asks.

"You can smell that, can't you?" Sandbrook asks Perry. Perry shrugs.

"What?" Ryk asks again. "I don't smell anything."

"Hmm, "Sandbrook responds with a smile. "I see. Perhaps it could have been my imagination," he adds; "or just maybe I did smell something."

"Perhaps," Ryk answers, looking confused.

"You will contact us should you remember or discover any further information related to the man's disappearance, won't you?" Sandbrook asks Ryk.

"Of course," Ryk answers, shaking his head somewhat anxiously.

Agent Sandbrook and Inspector Perry leave the bar with satisfied smirks on their faces.

Chapter 49

Creed stares off into the sky as he stands silently in front of a group of newly arrived, naked prisoners.

"Sir," Boron interrupts the silence; "as you were saying?"

"Yes," Creed responds, snapping from his distant gaze; "you won't be leaving here, none of you piss roaches, so get that through your piss-roach brains. This place is what you make of it, within certain limits," he adds laughing. "You can either get with our program, or eat pig shit. It's your call. Now get these piss roaches out of my face.

"File out of here," a guard yells, looking confused by the quick dismissal.

"He could be dead," Boron tells Creed as the prisoners board a rusty shuttle.

"What makes you say that?" Creed asks.

"We lost the signal at the same time we saw smoke rise from a crematorium," Boron answers. "What if he was cremated?"

"It was the woman from the FCO on Shangdu," Creed suddenly says; "of course."

"Who?" Boron asks.

"The woman we saw leaving the funeral home," Creed replies.

The Legendary Escape of Captain Vandoc

"Do you think she has something to do with this?" Boron asks.

"We're gonna find out," Creed answers. "Prepare the ship. We're going back to Shangdu, only we're taking the entire crew this time. All twelve of them, with wands. We're going to hunt the son of a bitch down."

"The whole crew?" Boron asks. "Is that wise?"

"Do I have to remind you of what they'll do to us if he shows up again before we get to him?" Creed asks. "We won't tell the crew what they're looking for, just that our camp was identified in a recent false alarm and we are returning to the area to conduct a test for trace elements. Tell them to maintain radio silence."

"They'll draw a lot of attention," Boron says.

"Not if we send them in different directions and insist on discretion," Creed tells him. "They're loyal."

"They're idiots," Boron replies.

"Loyal idiots," Creed replies. "With that many wands, we'll be able to triangulate his position. If he's there, we'll find him," he adds. "We'll find him and we'll get out."

Chapter 50

Lumina stops scrolling through data and smiles as she stares into her computer screen. She begins reciting numbers to herself, memorizing them. She has found something.

"A Colonel Creed is arriving at Bay 3 in ten minutes," an automated voice sounds over the sound system.

"What does he want?" Lumina inquires.

"Personal consultation," the voice replies.

Lumina walks to Bay 3, where she watches Creed's ship touch down. Within seconds, Creed and Boron step off the vessel.

"Welcome back to Shangdu, gentlemen," Lumina tells them. "How can I be of assistance?" she asks.

"We saw you in New Shangdu," Creed replies; "coming out of a funeral home."

"Yes," Lumina responds. "I thought that was you."

"Why were you there?" Boron asks.

"That's her business," Creed snaps.

"I was just there to visit the operator of the establishment," Lumina replies. "He's a member of our local church."

"You're Pawani, aren't you?" Creed asks.

"Yes, I am," Lumina answers.

"And where is your church?" Creed asks.

"It's located outside of New Shangdu," Lumina answers, hoping to conceal her village; "along the Orkhon River."

"So, you don't live in New Shangdu?" Boron asks.

"That's correct," Lumina answers, well aware of the dangers of lying to a military officer.

"Do you often come to the city to visit your funeral-directing friend?" Creed asks.

"No, not often," Lumina answers. "We had just celebrated our New Year and I came to thank him for the tireless work he did for our community. Now, how does this relate to your visit?" she asks.

"You might recall that there was a police alarm that sounded in New Shangdu," Creed responds. "We're here to figure out what the issue was."

"I would think the police alarm to be a police matter," Lumina says. "I guess I'm a little surprised to see the military involved."

"Any public safety matter may involve the military," Creed responds. "I wish I could tell you more, but we're not at liberty to discuss our objectives. We do appreciate your time, however. Now, if you'll excuse us, we have work to do."

"I wish you luck with that," Lumina says.

They stand in an awkward moment of silence.
Finally, Creed and Boron turn to walk to their ship.
Just before reaching the boarding ramp, Creed turns.

"What was the name of your town?" he yells to Lumina.

"Excuse me?" she asks.

"Your town on the river," Creed says. "What is its name?"

"Noradox," Lumina answers reluctantly.

With composure, she respectfully waits for Creed's ship to lift off. Once out of sight, she immediately calls Lok.

"What's up?" Lok answers.

"He's back," Lumina tells him; "that creep Colonel Creed and his even creepier sidekick. They just left here. They're looking for the captain and I think they're on their way to Noradox."

"Here?" Lok shouts. "How did they find out about us?"

"I had no choice," Lumina answers. "They saw us at the Pyre."

"We have to get him out of here," Lok says. "It won't take them long to cover this town with their wands."

"Get him to the caves," Lumina says. "Go now! Tell him I'll bring supplies by later this evening."

"Got it," Lok replies.

"Lok," Lumina says; "I think I have found a way to get him back to Kublai."

"Good, because that may be our only hope of getting out of this mess," Lok replies.

Within minutes, Lok and Vandoc arrive at Noradox Village train station. Lok buys two tickets to Shoreside Station; the closest stop to the caves. Vandoc stays out of sight. They board their train just as another train pulls into the station with two of Creed's crew members on board. Both crew members' wands light up simultaneously. One of them immediately calls Creed.

"What do you have?" Creed asks.

"A signal at Noradox Village train station," his goon answers as they step onto the platform.

"Stay right there," Creed replies. "We're on our way."

"Wait!" the crewman says just as Lok and Vandoc's train pulls away from the station. "We've lost the signal." They look around, but only see a train leaving the station. "I think the signal came from a train that's headed toward New Shangdu."

"You guys remain in Noradox and let me know if you detect anything," Creed instructs them. "I want everyone else to patrol all stations and main entry points into New Shangdu."

Vandoc and Lok get off at Shoreside, where Lok guides the captain to the river.

"I can take it from here," Vandoc tells him once the ocean comes into view. "I'll be in the northernmost cave of the large inlet," he says pointing to a distant cliff.

"I'll be back tonight with a few supplies," Lok tells him. "Lay low for now."

"Roger that," the captain says just before turning to the shoreline and vanishing into heavy vegetation.

Chapter 51

Creed and Boron stand on Platform Nine of New Shangdu's Riverside Station watching the Orkhon Corridor Shuttle arrive. Both try to be as discreet as possible as they continue checking their wands for a signal. They walk the length of the platform. Nothing is detected. Creed pulls his fon out and calls his crew member back.

"Are you certain it was the only shuttle?" Creed asks.

"Yes," his lacky answers; "only local trains stop in the piss-roach village."

"Well," Creed responds; "it just arrived and nothing is being detected."

"It was a local," Boron tells Creed. "He may have gotten off at another station."

"Or he may not even exist," Creed says angrily.

"True," Boron responds; "but not a safe bet to make.

"Search Noradox thoroughly," Creed instructs his crew member. "Tell these other idiots to spread out and patrol," he instructs Boron. "When at rest, they should remain near ports and maglev stations, in case we pick up a signal."

As the sun sets, Lumina arrives at Vandoc's cave.

"How did you get here so soon?" Vandoc asks.

"I came directly from work," Lumina answers. "I had to. I think I have a way to get you home and I had to memorize a few details to avoid recording them. I can't be linked to this."

"Tell me," Vandoc says wide-eyed.

"A high-level dignitary, most likely a cabinet member, is going to be flown tomorrow from the Port of New Shangdu to Kublai," Lumina answers. "Nobody knows that I know this. I can get you on that flight using a maintenance override code."

"How do you know this?" Vandoc asks her.

"It's often speculated throughout the Kingdom that high ranking members of the Khan's court travel anonymously for fear of assassination, usually via freight liners largely to avoid people," she answers; "usually in posh, private customized containers that can be shipped amidst cargo without crews even knowing they're on board."

"So, how do you know this is going to go down?" Vandoc asks.

"I figured out what they were doing long ago through patterns in the shipping records. Though periodic, it has happened several times," Lumina answers. "They reschedule times and routes in a manner that is inconsistent with typical changes. When you've seen as many scheduled shipments as I have, you develop a keen eye for detail. This one is crystal clear because it has been diverted to Kublai, and just prior to the Double Moon festival too."

"So how can I pull this off?" Vandoc asks.

"Remember this code," Lumina tells him; "7852MV-97P." She repeats it three times.

Soon, Vandoc is repeating it with her; "7852MV-97P."

"Here's a jacket that I grabbed from our maintenance room. Wear it," Lumina tells him. "The code you've just memorized will access both the facility entrance and the ship, which is operated by Regal Freight. It will be docked in berth 12. You will not have any reserved seat or quarters, so you'll have to keep moving while on board. Crew members seldom know each other, so anonymity works to your advantage."

"Will the ship dock in the Neutral Zone upon arrival?" Vandoc asks.

"No," Lumina answers; "but near it and within the deepest check-point. I've mapped out a course. Upon arrival, go to the front of the ship where you'll see a ramp leading off the side of the platform. There is a metal ladder. Climb down that ladder one level. You'll have clearance but no business being there. Don't run, but waste no time. A Shorebok ship is scheduled to be docked there at that time. If what you're saying is true, you should be able to access the ship from that platform, so long as they haven't changed their access code," she adds.

"They haven't in years and years," Vandoc answers.

"Here is a sleeping bag and pillow," Lumina says as she gives him a small pack. "There're some snacks, toiletries, and a few items to get you on your way. Also, here is Kyper's fon. There are still some monetary units on it in the event of an emergency. Do not call anyone on it. You could be signing their death warrants. Furthermore, it's traceable and trackable, so get rid of it at the first sign of trouble. Also, do not answer any call with a known source. Should we call you, we'll do so with a scrambler. Answer, but wait for me or Lok to speak first. If you hear us call you directly by name, meaning Kyper, assume the call is compromised, or at least not private. In that case, drop the call immediately, destroy your fon, and flee, for you can also assume the call has been traced. If the call is secure, I will simply call you 'cousin' instead of using your real name. Oh my God, what is your real name?" Lumina asks, realizing this may be the last time they meet.

"Vandoc," the captain replies. Lumina smiles.

"The flight departs at the midday hour tomorrow," she says. "It'll take three to four hours to reach the port from here on foot, but if you leave at dawn and follow the shoreline into New Shangdu, you should be there with time to spare. Remember to enter the facilities through the northern lot entrance.

"I'm going home," Vandoc says with a smile. "God, I can't tell you how grateful I am to you, Lok, and Forbin. I will spend my remaining days searching for ways to repay you."

"Don't get ahead of yourself," Lumina replies. "You're still a long way from home, Vandoc."

The two catch themselves gazing again into each other's eyes. The attraction between them is palpable and as strong as the moment they met. Finally, they break their gaze. Lumina looks down as a tear rolls down her cheek. She then just turns and walks away without the slightest of leave-takings. Vandoc watches her fade into the shoreline. She doesn't look back.

Chapter 52

Excited, Vandoc is up well before the dawn. He hastily decides to start making his way up the shoreline before the day's first light, using reflected moonlight off the Orkhon's surface to guide him. "I'm going home," he says to himself with a smile. "This has got to work."

He's almost an hour into his trek by the time the first hint of dawn arrives. The increasing light makes it somewhat easier for him to see, but also riskier, for he could now also be seen. The morning is in its infancy and little stirs at this hour. Vandoc quietly picks up his pace, following a trodden but overgrown footpath along the river's edge, utilizing the remaining darkness.

A smile comes over his face when he reaches the great fork in the river. He now knows where he is, nearing the midpoint of his hike. The early start has put him well ahead of schedule. He takes a moment to view the vast red sky and the golden reflection of a fading moon on the river's surface.

Creed and Boron stand just outside Riverside Station.

"The sun will be up soon," Boron tells Creed. "It's almost morning here. Might I remind you that we really don't blend in here."

"Shut up, Boron," Creed says; "I have a call to take. What is it?" he asks into his fon. "Venture out but stay in the vicinity of the station," he says. "Let me know if you pick up another signal."

"What is it?" Boron asks as Creed hangs up.

"We picked up a new signal at Fork Station," Creed says.

"Let's go," Boron says.

"They lost it," Creed says.

"Was he on a train?" Boron asks.

"There were no trains at the station at the time," Creed tells him. "He may be on foot. What are the closest Orkhon Corridor Shuttle stops to Fork?" he asks.

"Shoreside and Cliffview Stations," Boron replies.

"Send a team to Shoreside. Let's get to Cliffview," Creed says. "I've got a sneaking suspicion he could be trying to get back to New Shangdu."

Vandoc follows the Orkhon through a network of narrows. The trails soon separate from the river as it drops into a canyon. He climbs a steep catwalk along the inner cliff wall. The dawn has grown lighter but a thick fog has begun to accumulate around the river, diffusing the morning light and giving the captain a perfect blanket under which to escape.

Atop the cliff and just down a country road, however, Creed and Boron cut through that fog in a b-line for the river.

"I told you he wouldn't be in the station," Creed tells Boron. "Look, I'm getting a slight signal again. If he's on foot, we'll get him," he adds, gripping his rifle.

"If it's him, should we take him out?" Boron asks.

"No, how about we take him to dinner and a movie?" Creed responds, shaking his head.

Vandoc reaches the top of the cliff, where he finds himself along the maglev tracks. Cliffview Station can't be far, he thinks. Then he sees two flashlights approaching. Their beams cut through the fog as they scan the landscape, as if to be looking for something or someone. Not taking any chances, the captain stays low to avoid detection. With few options, he climbs beneath the tracks into the rusty framework of a bridge above an underpass, hoping the flashlights will move along.

"Look how strong the signal is," Boron says. "He's near."

"Cut the lights," Creed says.

The captain can now hear them. His eyes roll, then close in disbelief as he recognizes Creed's voice. With all the strength he can gather, he pulls himself onto an I-beam that sits just beneath the tracks. He cuts both of his hands severely in the act. "Son of a bitch," he yells in his head as he remains perfectly still, braced beneath the bridge, dripping blood from both of his hands.

"Look at that," Boron says; "that reading just shot off the meter."

"Captain Vandoc," Creed yells. "If you can hear me, I'm giving you a chance to surrender peacefully. We have you surrounded and more men are on their way. If you make this easier on us, we'll make it easier on you."

At this very moment, sheep begin to pass beneath the captain; an entire herd followed by an elderly shepherd with a tall, hooked walking stick. Neither the sheep nor the shepherd glance upward, leaving the captain unnoticed. Blood continues to drip from the captain's injured hands, now landing on sheep as they pass beneath him.

"He's on the move," Vandoc hears Boron yell. Silence ensues.

"WT Fuck?" he then hears Creed yell.

"Is he hiding with the sheep?" he hears Boron ask.

"No, sheep brain," Creed replies shaking his head. "He's in a volcano back on Pyro," he yells as they follow the herd further down the road with flashlights.

The captain dresses his wound, then slips into the fog, down the tracks to Cliffview Station. Once there, he removes the bloody cloth and begins tearing it into pieces. Along the way, he tosses one piece of the cloth into the open window of a city bus, then drops another smaller piece into the tire grooves of a parked police cycle. He tosses the last piece into the trash in the station's men's room before continuing on his way down the tracks toward New Shangdu.

Chapter 53

Once beyond the cliffs, Vandoc is able to follow the shoreline to New Shangdu. Direct sunlight has cracked the snow-capped peaks of a distant mountain range by the time he arrives at the city's port, the largest ship yard in the Kingdom. Massive freighters are moored as they load and fuel. He watches one lift off, climb, and disappear into the sky. Nervously, he takes a deep breath before entering the northern lot, knowing fear will only raise suspicion. With this in mind, Vandoc reminds himself not to think, just act.

Meanwhile, Creed and Boron stand beside Creed's ship. Boron is on his fon.

"Sir, the crew is picking up strong readings around Cliffview Station," Boron tells Creed.

"So did we," Creed replies; "and it turned out to be sheep. Tell them to return to ship. We have to get the hell out of here before this story explodes."

As Boron tells the crew to return, a police sensor is tripped, sounding a repetitive alarm around Cliffview Station. Creed overhears it through Boron's fon.

"Goddamn it," he yells; "tell those peons to get their asses back to the ship right now! We're lifting off."

Back at the port, Vandoc gains composure as he walks to the entrance and keys in 7852MV-97P. A green-light blinks as the door unlatches. The captain enters. Inside, he finds berth 12 to be empty.

"Can we help you find something," Vandoc hears a voice behind him say. He turns to see two huge guys, both wearing identical sunglasses."

"I was told I could catch my ship here," the captain tells them; "to Kublai."

"Who are you?" the taller of the two guys asks.

"Maintenance," Vandoc answers.

"Go over there," the man replies; "where all those guys are standing. It should arrive any moment." Vandoc nods and follows his direction.

He finds himself standing in a group of crew members, all waiting for the ship's arrival.

"What's up with those guys?' a food service worker asks him. "They've been around here all morning. And now we've been diverted to Kublai."

"What can you do?" Vandoc asks, shrugging his shoulders.

Moments later, a massive cargo liner descends from the sky. Everyone watches its retro rockets fire as it softly comes to rest on the platform. Soon, a door opens and all the workers walk onto the vessel, including Captain Vandoc. He smiles at the ease of it, not even having to enter his code again. Once on board, he brakes from the group and makes his way to the cargo hold, where he finds a secluded spot to ponder his next move.

Suddenly, the lights begin to dim and brighten, repeatedly at steady intervals, alerting the crew that lift off is near. A few minutes later, the outboard engines fire up, causing the massive vessel to vibrate. Vandoc laughs as the ship begins to lift off the ground.

Chapter 54

Creed's ship sub-surfaces through the ceiling of Pyro's dark clouds, then glides around Mt. Dyvok on approach.

"I think he's on Shangdu," Boron tells creed.

The Legendary Escape of Captain Vandoc

"He's in that volcano, right there," Creed replies as he points to Dyvok.

"Why are all the signal signatures pointing to our camp?" Boron asks.

"How should I know?" Creed asks back.

"He booked himself on a live shipment to Shangdu," Boron says.

"Which he wasn't on," Creed replies. "Interplanetary travel is strictly monitored in this system. It's not like he can hitchhike. I think you're getting paranoid."

"Or you're in denial," Boron suggests. "Our asses are so on the line here."

The ship sets down on its private platform at Creed's quarters. Creed and Boron swiftly disembark, followed by the crew. Once inside, they're immediately notified of an incoming call from Commander Nerabo.

"Take it," Creed instructs as he takes a seat on his thrown.

"What in Sam-fuck is occurring on Shangdu, Creed?" Nerabo asks.

"Another alarm?" Creed asks, acting stupid.

"Try three," Nerabo answers.

"Oh," Creed says; "of course. It must have been the group I sent to the Iridium Diggers Convention."

"I'm not in the mood for humor," Nerabo replies.

"What do you want me to say?" Creed responds. "For God's sake, how would I know what is happening on Shangdu?"

"The signatures all point to Pyro," Nerabo tells him; "with impeccable precision."

"It blows my mind too," Creed says, making a mind-blown gesture with his hands.

"If there's something to this, Creed," Nerabo says; "they will hang us both on Good Morning Kingdom."

"Love the show," Creed replies. "Did you get the spirits I sent?"

"Fuck yourself," Nerabo says just before cutting the connection.

Chapter 55

Still in the cargo hold, Vandoc shivers as he sits on the ground between stacks of containers. He decides to walk around among the containers to raise his core temperature. He is soon stopped, however, by the same two big guys in sunglasses back at the port.

"What are you doing in here?" the taller one asks.

"Working on a panel," Vandoc replies. "It's cold, so I thought I'd walk around a little to warm myself."

"Let the man be," a deep voice says from within an open container door. Seconds later, out steps none other than the Khan himself." Vandoc stands stunned. "Don't be alarmed," the Khan tells Vandoc. "I am a man of the people, of the common man," he adds as he walks up to the captain and looks him square in the eye. Do you have a camera?" he asks Vandoc.

"Yes, I do," the captain replies.

"Would you like to take a selfie together?" the Khan asks.

"Yes, I would," Vandoc replies."

The captain pulls his newly acquired fon out and lines up next to the Khan. They have to stand virtually cheek to cheek in order to frame both of their faces in the photo. Vandoc gets a pungent whiff of whiskey from the Khan's breath as he snaps the pic. The Khan laughs, then pats him on the back before simply turning around and disappearing back into his container, followed by his two goons, who shut the door and latch it behind them. Vandoc moves on, away from the container, shaking his head in utter shock.

Chapter 56

The colossal freighter begins to vibrate as it fires its retro-boosters, slowing to enter Kublai's atmosphere. Vandoc paces to stay warm. Through a small porthole he watches the ship glow as it first strikes the upper atmosphere. The view morphs from fire to cloud, then suddenly the Glass Sea. "Oh my God," Vandoc says as he looks out the window; "I'm back." This planet that once seemed so distant, now feels like home; Kublai.

The moment, however, also carries the weight of reality, for the captain understands not only how close he is, but how far. He has no contingency plan should the access code fail. There is no plan to be found. Evading arrest without even a map or any understanding of the port seems highly unlikely. He smiles nonetheless, for he operates on a belief, or a sense of divine energy within him. He wasn't made to fail here. His story needs to be told. And what about the winds that saved him on Pyro, or of encountering Lumina, and all the other breaks he's had? How could his luck run out now? It just wasn't meant to.

As the ship glides over the Glass Sea in its final approach, Vandoc returns to the crew entrance. There, several members are standing, waiting for the ship to touch down. He pulls his hood over his head. The ship soon sets down and the door opens. Go time has arrived.

Vandoc can feel his heart racing as he exits the ship. He keeps his head down, reducing exposure to any video surveillance. He glances suspiciously out of the corner of his eye, but everyone seems to be going about their own business. There appear to be no guards on the platform. He follows Lumina's plan to the letter, first going to the front of the ship, where he sees a ramp leading off the side of the platform. He walks down it swiftly and confidently. Sure enough, there it is; the metal ladder. He decides not to even look around as he steps onto it and begins climbing down. Near the end, however, he runs into a snag. There is a locked gate blocking the ladder's way. Oddly, he is able to climb around the gate via the railing, but looks conspicuously unauthorized doing so. He's between levels, however, and nobody seems to have noticed. Once back on the ladder, he finishes his descent to the lower level, now within the Neutral Zone.

As foretold, there sits a Shorebok Shipping freighter at the far end of the platform. There are a lot of workers on the platform, coming off ships or waiting for others to dock. The captain blends in as he makes his way to the freighter. He encounters an armed port agent on the way, but raises no suspicion. Could it be this easy?

Vandoc reaches the ship and looks down the platform. The agent is gone. He takes a deep breath and begins entering numbers on the ship's outer access pad. Once the numbers are entered, he hesitates for several seconds, then hits "enter." The panel turns red and flashes the message "INCORRECT ACCESS CODE." A loud repetitive alarm sounds from the ship. The captain takes one step back, turns, and simply walks away while the alarm continues to sound. He looks over his shoulder with an annoyed look on his face, as if he too was bothered by the alarm as he heads straight back to the ladder. To his surprise, nobody around seems to have noticed that he was the one to trip the alarm. Quickly, he scales the ladder and makes his way back up to the next level in the wake of the commotion, which for the moment remains localized. Security officers race to the scene below.

Once back on the upper level, he walks off of the platform with a group of laborers. They all flash ID tags to a security officer as they pass a checkpoint. The captain merely raises his arm as if he's holding one. The guard doesn't seem to notice. Two workers do, however, and scowl at the captain, but say nothing. They stop and wait at a service elevator, where the alarm can still be heard from below.

"What's going on down there?" one of them asks the group. Nobody answers.

The elevator arrives and Vandoc manages to board it with the first group. He sighs as the doors close. As they descend, however, he overhears the operator's radio mentioning enhanced exit checks on the ground level.

"I need off on Level Two," Vandoc asks the operator; "I forgot my tools." The same two guys who scowled at him for his lack of credentials now look livid. One of them shakes his head. They seem to know the captain is posing.

The elevator stops on two and Vandoc gets off, clueless to what he's stepping into. The doors close and he finds himself facing an extravagant entrance to the Ministry of Transport. A guard sits behind massive glass doors. The captain spots a men's room before the security check. He ducks into it.

Inside the washroom, a security guard is using the urinal. Vandoc disappears into a stall. He sits on the toilet waiting for the guard to leave. He hears a flush, the running of sink water, then nothing. He carefully steps out of the stall and over to a corner window. He opens it as far as it will open, but it remains well shy of his girth. There is a street light post below. He can hear sirens in the distance, soon followed by more. Desperately, he decides to kick the window open.

The sound of breaking glass carries further than he'd hoped. Vandoc climbs out onto a small sill, then steps gracefully out onto the top of the street lamp. When doing so, he loses his footing and slips. Luckily, he manages to grab the post as he falls but is unable to slow himself enough, striking the pavement below with a loud thud.

As sirens grow, Vandoc rises to his feet and limps into a garage, out of sight of the washroom window. He follows a vehicle ramp downward until he reaches street level, climbs over a handrail and out the side of the garage, avoiding traffic. To his surprise, he finds himself standing amidst parade spectators, celebrating the arrival of the first moon. He limps down the block with the parade and into the first open door he can find, into Kublai's Underground Museum. Once inside, he is stopped at the admission counter.

"It's thirty-five boyoos,"[5] the ticket agent tells him; "which includes full access to the museum and the underground tour." With no other option, Vandoc pulls Kyper's fon out and scans the payment code. A beep is heard and a light blinks green. "Payment accepted," it reads.

Vandoc enters the museum and heads straight to the gift shop, where he buys a shaving kit and some travel scissors, again using his new fon. Still limping, he takes the kit into the men's room and locks himself

---

[5] **boyoo**: the monetary unit of the Kingdom in 3255.

into a stall. Inside, he removes his maintenance hat
and jacket and begins cutting off all of his hair with the
small travel scissors. Once his hair is mostly gone,
he lathers his head with shaving foam and shaves
himself bald. When finished, he steps out of the stall
and in front of a sink, where he uses the jacket to
wipe off all remaining shaving foam. He stuffs the
shirt, hat and shaving kit into the trash.

Two police officers enter the lobby just as the captain
steps out of the washroom, hairless, prompting him to
join a small tour group listening to an exhibitor lecture
in the lobby.

"Were it not for these," the exhibitor says as he
plays with the dials on an ancient Falcon-3
transmitter; "there would be no Kingdom. The human
race would still be confined to the Solar System with
the possible exception of a few neighboring stars. We
would still be mired in radio communication."

"Were the Falcon models the first faster-than-
light transmitters?" Vandoc asks to look more
engaged in the discussion.

"No," the lecturer answers; "the first were
colonial. Falcon Transmissions improved upon
colonial technology, however," he adds.

Police file past them, showing a holographic image of
Vandoc crossing the platform. It's clear from a
distance but pixelates as they expand the 3D image.
The museum patrons wave the police off one by one,

including Vandoc when confronted. He subtly takes a deep breath after they pass, safely concealed for the moment by his new look.

"Does it work?" Vandoc asks the exhibitor.

"This one? I'm afraid not," the lecturer replies. "All it would need is a power converter to make it compatible with our modern grid. We just haven't had much use for it over the last few centuries. Why transmit a message that can't even outrun our slowest freighters today?" he asks the group. They smile at his delivery.

Still in pain from the pavement, Vandoc limps over to a very small movie theater within the museum.

"Are you going to take the underground tour?" a ticket agent asks while checking the captain's receipt. "The next one starts in fifteen minutes."

"I haven't decided," Vandoc answers.

"Well, this film explains the tour and gives a little history of Kublai City's ancient underground."

"I've read of it," Vandoc replies; "but know so little about it."

"This film is a great place to start," the agent suggests.

Vandoc nods and enters the room. The film is already playing. He sits toward the back and starts rubbing his knee.

"Why did Shorebok change the goddamned access code?" he mumbles to himself as he sits in the dark.

Chapter 57

"What if he escapes?" Nebula asks Nario as she sits on his lap in a sudsy sunken tub.

"He won't," Nario answers, sensually entranced. "Even if he did, he would have no way out of the Kingdom."

"What if he got to one of your ships?" Nebula asks.

"He'd be fresh out of luck," Nario answers.

"Oh, how so?" Nebula asks.

"I changed the access code."

"Won't that raise suspicion?" Nebula asks.

"Not as much as him gaining access to a ship," Nario replies. "Now stop worrying. He's gone."

Chapter 58

The captain closes his eyes and takes a deep breath as the film plays, well aware that he cannot linger.

"The city you and I know as Kublai," the film narration begins; "conceals a vastly different city; an ancient city of canals and waterways, many of which still flow beneath us today." Mystina Island appears in the film on an ancient map of the canals, to the north and well off the coast.

"Mystina Island," Vandoc quietly repeats. His eyes widen with thought. He looks carefully at the map of canals before it fades. "I've gotta get out of here." He gets up. With a less noticeable limp, he walks to the front of the theater, where he opens an exit door. The sound of sirens and flashing police lights fill the room. The captain quickly closes the door, turns around and returns to the lobby.

"I've decided to take the underground tour," he tells the ticket agent.

"You'll enjoy it," the agent replies. "It begins in five minutes and leaves from this lobby."

A screen in the lobby shows a yet clearer shot of Vandoc on the platform with the headline 'Assassination Attempt?' The broadcast flashes forward to a view of the men's room on the second floor of the Port Building. The camera moves to the window used in the escape and even focuses on the light pole. They're closing in fast.

"Good afternoon to all those joining us on the Underground Tour," a voice announces. "Please have your passes out and follow me." Vandoc patiently queues up, while itching deep down inside to make a run for it. A gate opens and the group follows the guide into a dark stairwell that takes them down to a cobblestone road beneath the city street. It crosses a canal via an ancient footbridge, into a ghostly city of stone buildings that make up the foundations of the modern city above them.

"Water built this city," the guide tells the group. "Unfortunately, it's also what destroyed it, forcing it to be built again above us."

Vandoc stays with the group, patiently waiting to reach Central Canal. The tour is fascinating, following a stone path lit with lanterns along ancient canals. They finally cross a footbridge over Central Canal. The captain slows his pace, acting distracted and allowing himself to fall behind the group. As they round a bend in the path, he turns around and starts to make his way back to the canal, now on his own. Once there, he drops down onto a small walkway that runs along the canal's edge, disappearing into the darkness.

The path soon comes to an end at an iron gate. The canal, however, runs beneath it. With no choice, the

captain climbs into the cold flowing water. He
manages to swing himself under the gate, holding
onto it as he stares at the raging current ahead. The
canal disappears into steamy fog between two stone
walls. Vandoc wishes he had better options, or even
an option. He tries to be as calm as possible,
breathing in deeply, then slowly letting it out. After
several breaths, he releases his grip on the gate and
lets the canal take him into the fog. Moving rapidly,
he kicks but cannot feel any bottom bed to this
current. Any effort to swim would be in vain. All he's
able to do is try to keep his head above water as he
moves swiftly below a city that is searching for him.

Things go from bad to worse for Vandoc as he
reaches a point where two channels merge, pulling
him into a small whirlpool. The current keeps sucking
him under, then spitting him back upward before
sucking him under again, and again. Just as he fears
he has taken his final breath, the whirlpool spits him
back into the current. With all the energy he has, he
manages to suspend himself for a moment by digging
his fingertips into a stone wall he flows past, but the
current soon pulls him back.

A massive set of iron doors close in front of the
captain. He slams into them before being pulled
backward by the current as the water begins to swirl.
He has entered a system of locks. Giant doors
behind him soon close as well, creating a chamber.
Suddenly, two large automated hatches spring open

on each side, releasing a sludgy substance. A powerfully pungent breeze of sheer ass follows, singeing the captains nose hairs.

"Real nice. Raw fucking sewage," Vandoc yells, trying not to draw a breath. "I don't have a stomach for this." He dry heaves as the chamber begins to fill with wastewater. The walls are metallic and slick, leaving him with nothing to grab onto. The water quickly rises as the chamber floods. Treading waste-water is all the he can do to stay afloat, still subject to the current's course.

There is a moment of silence once the chamber stops filling, but then its front doors open, pulling the captain into the reservoir of a dam. He swims for its rocky shoreline but finds he's being pulled backward, toward the dam. Soon realizing his struggle is futile, he turns to see his inevitable course. Ahead, he spots a vortex in the water. He's going under. He decides not to wait to be pulled under, takes a deep breath and swims downward to look for options. He sees what's pulling him; a massive underwater culvert. He can also see a school of fish moving through a fish ladder. He resurfaces and swims toward the ladder. He gets closer to it, surfaces, then submerges again. He can see some kids watching the fish migrate through an aquarium window. One of the kids notices the captain and points him out to a friend.

The current behind the captain is too powerful, pulling him closer to the culvert. He barely manages to surface long enough to draw a deep breath before being pulled under again. Realizing there is no fighting it, he swims right at the culvert. It quickly sucks him into a pipeline. As he accelerates, the captain tucks himself into a ball, knowing he could be diced in a turbine at any moment. He releases his last breath. On the verge of passing out, he is sprayed out of the face of the dam in a raging stream of pressurized water. While freefalling well over a hundred meters, Vandoc manages to pull in another deep breath just before slamming deeply into the water. Barely conscious, he swims for the surface, only to be slammed yet deeper and deeper by the weight of the waterfall. Out of breath, he swims sideways beneath the current as far as he can before giving the surface another shot.

Vandoc gasps desperately for air as he surfaces downriver from the dam, still moving swiftly with the stream. An old man stares at him from the bank as he drifts uncontrollably by. He is soon, however, able to grab hold of a vine, gain footing, and climb to the river's shore. There, he just sits on a large stone under light falling rain, catching his breath. In front of him, he can see it; the Glass Sea.

Chapter 59

A military drone soars slowly over the coastline. To avoid detection, Vandoc steps away from the entrance of his rocky den within the walls of Kublai's sea-cliffs. He's naked, waiting for his clothes to dry by a small fire that he lit with his laser starter; one of the few items he kept from his pack.

"This is the Kublai Police Department," a scrambled message reads on Vandoc's fon. "Turn yourself in to avoid severe punishment." The captain knows not to answer, for scrambled signals cannot be traced unless he connects. It does tell him, however, that the police have identified him, or Kyper Corlox for that matter. He can no longer turn on his fon, nor access its wallet.

When darkness drops, he makes his way northward, staying along the coast, out of sight. He walks throughout the moonlit night; the night of the arrival of the second moon. Just before the break of dawn, he encounters a marina. Two rough looking fishermen are loading a small fishing vessel. Vandoc approaches them.

"Are you guys going anywhere near Mystina Island?" the captain asks them. They both laugh as they continue loading their boat. "I can pay you in square root," Vandoc adds. They stop loading.

"What do you have?" the older of the two men asks. Vandoc pulls out a packet of Creed's square root; something else that he has kept since the night he escaped, knowing it could become his only currency. The men's eyes widen at the sight of it,

"Where did you get that?" the younger one asks. "That's VIP packaging."

"It's imperial grade," Vandoc tells them. "I have two packets. You can have them both. I just want you to take me to Mystina Island."

"I'm Admiral Crow and this is Captain Nok," the older of the two fisherman says. "Welcome aboard, but stay beneath the quarter deck. Mystina's an hour off shore. Oh, and we'll take one of the packets now as a down payment, and the other upon arrival."

"Fair enough," the captain replies as he hands over a packet and boards the ship. Beneath the quarter deck, he finds a padded bench. He lies on it. Some stars can still be seen in the dark morning sky as his ship to Mystina sets sail. No bench has ever felt better, he thinks as he begins to drift to sleep.

Vandoc rudely awakens after suddenly being thrown against the bench's backrest by a sudden shift in the ship's direction. Another shift in the opposite direction throws him off the bench. He rises and staggers as he tries to get on deck to see what's going on. Once there, he finds Admiral Crow and Cpt. Nok laughing hysterically, both heavily intoxicated.

"Did you guys take the root?" Vandoc asks.

"Look who's here," the admiral yells. "They're coming after you," he tells Vandoc, as he points to a light in the fog on the water's horizon.

"It's not moving," Vandoc answers. "It's a stationary light, not a vessel."

"You lie," the admiral screams as he brandishes a gun. "They want you. You have to get out of here before they take us down too."

"What are you talking about?" Vandoc asks. "Listen, it's the square root talking. NO-BO-DY is out there. Just get me to Mystina, please, and I will get out of here. I promise you'll never see me again."

"You're lying. Get the hell off my boat," Crow screams as he shoots the gun, grazing Vandoc's ear.

"Okay, fuck, okay," Vandoc yells, pressing his

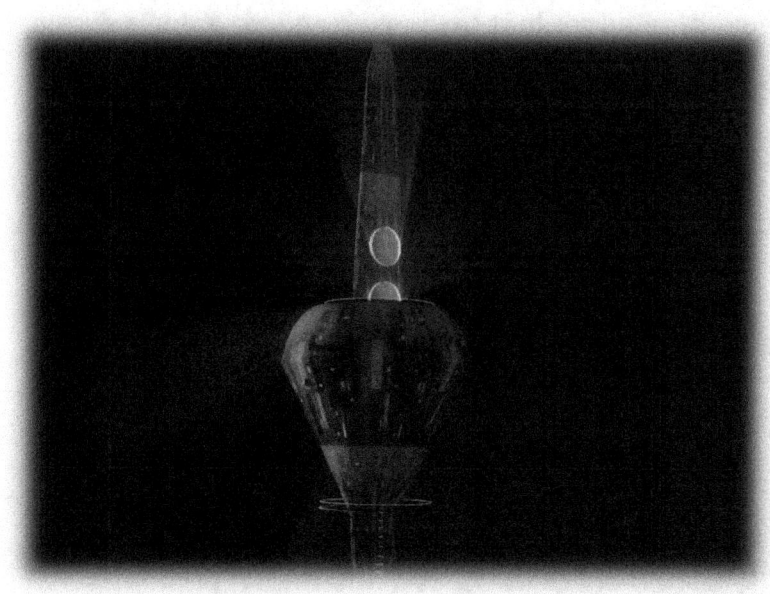

hand against his bleeding ear. He takes a look around and sees nothing but the single light on the horizon. He dives into the water and begins swimming toward it.

He can hear the two men laughing as their boat fades into the fog, still moving erratically. He swims for the light through not only the darkness, but a sea known throughout the galaxy for its horrific creatures. As the light grows closer, he can see that it is elevated, on a tower. Soon, the shape of an offshore carbon regulator appears in the fog; a tower used for the ongoing terraforming of the planet.

"I can make it," Vandoc says to himself as he gasps for air. He hears a sound in the water behind him. Something is following him. He presses on. Soon, he reaches the tower. Out of breath, he grabs hold of a ladder that extends from the water's surface up the tower's side. Just as he's about to pull himself up, however, a massive slithering beast's head emerges from the water, locks onto the captain's foot with one bite, and pulls him back into the water, beneath the surface. Vandoc resurfaces for air as the serpent releases his bite, but is again pulled under by one of the beast's tentacles after it wraps itself around the captain's legs. Vandoc grabs hold of the tower's ladder beneath the surface as the creature tries to make off with him. The beast tugs and tugs to get him to loosen his grip but the captain holds fast, finally managing to pull himself free between tugs. He uses the ladder to pull himself quickly to the surface. He climbs out of the ocean and onto a platform panting desperately for air. The creature surfaces below him, trying in vain to slither up the side of the tower wall, but soon disappears beneath the water's crest.

The captain lies on his back catching his breath, safe for now but stuck in the middle of nowhere.

Chapter 60

"Is this book any good?" Inspector Perry asks, pointing to a floating screen above Agent Sandbrook's desk. The image is of the cover of Commadore Trebok's book.

"I just finished it," Sandbrook replies; "and yes, it's fascinating. There is no direct mention of any black hole in the book, but he did run into a gravitational anomaly that pulled him off course during a mission. He was fortunate enough to correct it just in time."

"So, you think it's Notorbok?" Perry asks.

"It might be," Sandbrook answers. "It happened when Trebok was on a mission beneath the galactic plane, to Pondo."

"Agent Sandbrook," a soft, automated female voice calls over the sound system; "Agent Carlton is here to see you."

"Let him in," Sandbrook replies. "Noria," he adds; "what is our closest Sagittarian outpost to the planet Pondo?"

"We have a functioning communication post in orbit around the planet Cubikos," she answers.

"How often do we receive updates from there?" Sandbrook asks.

"Monthly," she answers. "It hasn't seen much action since the conflict."

"Let's increase that to hourly," Sandbrook instructs. "I want that station and any others within a three-thousand light year vicinity of it put on full alert."

An unshaven, scruffy looking guy enters the room. Sandbrook invites him to sit down.

"What do you have for us, Agent Carlton?" Sandbrook asks.

"Our intelligence sources say there may have been an assassination attempt of the Khan," Carlton answers.

"How does another assassination attempt merit you making a trip to deliver this news personally?" Sandbrook asks.

"The alleged assassin tried to board a colonial ship in Kublai's Neutral Zone," Carlton answers. "And get a load of this," he adds; "he tried to board a Shorebok Shipping freighter using an access code that failed."

Sandbrook smiles, stroking his beard.

Chapter 61

The fog's ceiling drops as morning starlight heats the sky. Remnants of a mighty volcano appear above the low swirling cloud-line; Mystina Island. It doesn't look that far away either, but hard to gauge with its shoreline enshroud by the thinning blanket of fog over the Glass Sea. There is no sign of the sea beast, but the captain doesn't find that very reassuring. Swimming for the shore seems like suicide, but so does staying on this platform. Cautiously, he climbs down the ladder to the water's surface.

Mystina's shore fades in and out of view through the fog. There it is, so near and yet so far. He continues down the ladder, now beneath the water's surface. He looks around the tower base but sees nothing stirring. He resurfaces, then quietly begins swimming on his back in Mystina's direction. The tower's base soon disappears in the fog, leaving only a view of the silhouetted platform. Vandoc rolls over and starts a crawl. A few short minutes later, he pulls up to tread water. The tower now looks so far away, and so does the island. Exhausted, Vandoc now fears he may not have what it takes to make the shore. He rolls onto his back and treads water, then starts again toward the island, breathing steadily but heavily.

Then he hears it; an evil hissing sound behind him. A moment later, he feels something wrap around his ankle. The grip tightens just before it pulls him several meters under water, then releases him. Desperate for air, Vandoc swims back to the surface, drawing a deep breath just in time to be pulled under again. This time, he finds himself staring into the eyes of the beast. Again, he is let go. With all the energy he's got, the captain again swims for the surface, almost unconscious. He makes it to the crest but knows he'll never have the energy to reach the shore, which he can no longer see. His predator won't let it happen, anyway. He's playing with his prey.

Vandoc gets four deep breaths in before being pulled under again, this time much deeper. His eardrums almost rupture from the sudden shift in pressure. Looking up, he can barely see the water's crest. He starts upward but begins to faint as he ascends. Just as his vision goes black, he feels his own shirt pull him upward. He sees a light growing brighter.

Suddenly, he is able to feel air. He coughs water out of his lungs and draws a deep breath. Something is suspending him, pushing him upward from beneath the surface. He ducks beneath the crest again to see not only two massive bottlenose dorca[6] working in concert to keep him afloat, but six others in a circle around them, facing outward to form a defensive perimeter. The sea creature slithers around the pod for a several seconds before disappearing into the deep.

The dorcas continue to push the exhausted captain in the direction of Mystina, almost to the beach before their pod simply swims onward. Vandoc's weak breaststroke takes him closer until he finds that he is able to stand and walk ashore. He sits on the shore amid driftwood, on the dead trunk of an ancient tree, staring at the top of what used to be midway up Mt. Mystina, before it blew that is.

Chapter 62

Meanwhile, orbiting high above Mars, Inspector Perry and Agent Sandbrook sit in a café within the ringway, watching ships decelerate. Nario Shorebok enters.

---

[6] **Dorca Whale**: a cross between an orca and a dolphin.

"Thank you for joining us," Sandbrook tells Nario as he motions for him to take a seat.

"I'm happy to help," Nario says with a strong hint of scepticism. "I heard you were in New Kublai," he adds.

"Isn't that impressive," Sandbrook tells Perry. "Now we know news travels fast, because we just got back ourselves, and we know that we traveled fast."

"The news beat us back," Inspector Perry replies with a grin.

"Speaking of news," Sandbrook tells Nario; "we may have some good news ourselves."

"You don't say," Nario responds. "Do tell."

"Take a look at this image," Sandbrook tells him as he displays a security camera image of Vandoc trying to access the Shorebok ship in Kublai's Neutral Zone.

"What am I looking at?" Nario asks.

"Do you know him?" Sandbrook asks.

"No, should I?" Nario asks. "I can't make much out from this image."

"I see," Sandbrook says. "Do you recognize the ship?"

"It looks like a freighter," Nario answers.

"It is," Sandbrook responds; "and it's one of yours."

The Legendary Escape of Captain Vandoc

"Yes," Nario replies, realizing he can only play so dumb; "I did get word that someone tried to access one of our ships in the Neutral Zone. Is that what this is about?"

"Why were they unable to do so?" Sandbrook asks.

"They didn't have the code," Nario answers.

"I see," Sandbrook replies; "and what code did the man in this image enter?"

"I don't know," Nario answers.

"We would like to," Sandbrook says. "Have you changed the code recently?" he asks.

"I don't recall," Nario answers. "I issue a lot of directives."

"So, if the code was changed recently, it would have to have been approved by you," Sandbrook says as he takes notes; "and you don't recall if you approved any such change as of late," he says as he jots information onto his screen.

"Like I said, I have to approve a lot of things," Nario responds.

"Mr. Shorebok," Sandbrook says; "we would like to speak with whoever works in your office, directly under you. I'm sure someone can help us answer our questions," he adds, smiling at Perry.

"Let me save you the trouble, gentlemen," Nario replies as he puts his earpiece in to make a private call. "Now what questions exactly would you like to have answered?"

"We would like to know when the code was last changed; when it had last been changed prior to this most recent change; and if the code used that set off the alarm matches any previous code," Sandbrook tells him with a dead serious look in his eyes.

"Let me make a call," Nario replies. He stands up and steps away from the table for a few minutes, talking into his earphone. A few minutes later, he returns. "The code was changed last week," he tells the agents.

"And the last time before that?" Perry asks him.

"Nine years," Nario answers.

"And the code that tripped the alarm?" Sandbrook asks.

"It matched a previous code," Nario answers.

"I'm assuming it was the one that existed just prior to last week," Sandbrook says, shaking his head. "How timely," he adds.

"Well, thank god we changed it," Nario tells them; "and just in the nick of time!"

"Yes, curiously," Sandbrook repeats as he smiles at Nario.

"You don't think it was Captain Vandoc, do you?" Nario asks. "That picture doesn't even look like him," he adds. "Vandoc isn't that thin and doesn't have that long of hair."

"You mean he *wasn't* and he *didn't*," Perry replies. "Under his circumstance, weight loss and hair growth are both indeed plausible."

"We don't know who is in that picture," Sandbrook responds. "We don't like to put the cart in front of the horse, so to speak. We just have these dots to connect, and we will."

"Well, I certainly hope it is him," Nario says, "though I wouldn't want to be on the run in the Kingdom."

"If it is him," Sandbrook says with a nod and a smile; "my money is on him getting out."

Chapter 63

The beach becomes a meadow on Vandoc's trek to the volcano. Dreamily, he walks through it, hungry and sleep deprived but smiling. The landscape is layered in meadow, mist, mountain, and sky. He is high on relief from the continual channel of adrenaline that has flown down his spine for days.

His relief is short lived, however, as he begins to hear a distant rumbling sound. The mountain couldn't be waking up today, could it? The rumbling grows. It's been dormant for millions of years, he thinks. His rationale, however, quickly crumbles when he spots the source of the sound; a massive four-legged beast bearing a single front horn, apparently charging him.

"Goddamn, what next?" he yells as he breaks for a treeline on the edge of the meadow. He arrives and disappears into the trees just before the beast rolls over the final hill and into the meadow, still headed straight at him. The trees are unique and foreign to him. Fortunately, they are easily scaled. Vandoc jumps onto one with a low branch and quickly climbs to a lofty height, hoping that whatever is coming his way can't climb. He can again feel adrenaline run down his spine as he tensely awaits his fate.

The trees begin to shake just before the thunderous beast emerges on the scene. It zigzags through the trees, snorting, shredding the ground beneath its feet, all without noticing the captain. Vandoc takes a deep breath and turns to the sky, waiting for the animal to move on. After a very long minute, the sound fades, then disappears.

Vandoc climbs from the tree and makes his way toward the base of the mountain, now hoping to get to higher ground soon. He comes upon a clearing where a cliff overlooks a rapidly flowing river. On the other side of the river, he can see giant woolly mammoths picking some kind of fruit from the trees.

Suddenly, the unicornic beast reappears from the trees, leaving the captain trapped along the cliff's edge. The animal begins to scrape the ground with its right-front hoof, itching to charge. Vandoc backs to the edge of the cliff. The beast lunges, forcing the captain to jump for the river from the cliff wall. He makes the water but is quickly swept into a swift current. Managing to keep his head above water, he gets pulled downstream. The river soon slows around a bend, giving him a chance to grab the edge of a stone and climb out, right next to a woolly mammoth drinking from the bank. On the distant cliff, silhouetted by the final remnants of morning fog, the angry horned beast bellows at the fading moons. The angry animal seems to draw the attention of someone or something else, for Vandoc spots a flash of light from the distant rim of the volcano, too bright for any natural source.

Initially frightened by the mammoth, Vandoc soon realizes that it has neither an interest in nor a fear of him. He gathers some wood, pulls his fire starter from his pocket and gets a small fire going along a protective river inlet. He strips naked, rings his clothes out and lays them on dry rocks in the morning sun. The mammoth draws curiously nearer when it sees his fire.

"Well, here I am in prehistoric times," he tells the massive mastodon. "What in the name of god was that thing on the other side of the river?" The mammoth remains expressionless.

Once his clothes dry, Vandoc dresses. He bids a fond adieu to his new woolly pal and presses onward. He hikes all afternoon before making the rim of the crater. The view is clear. He follows a coulee downward, into the crater, toward an ancient lake that lies at its center. The coulee soon merges with a spring. The captain follows it, past a waterfall, down to the lake.

At the lake, he gathers wood, doing his best to prepare for the night. He gets a fire going just as the sun sets on the rim of the crater, forming a halo-like glow in the misty air. A sense of safety comes over the captain as he sits in silence. He begins to wonder how true it is. What are the odds of this Shadow Fleet even existing, let alone being here on this island?

"Hey fleet, fleet, fleet,   " he screams from the top of his lungs. He listens as echoes bounce off distant inner crater walls, stirring birds from trees. "I'm here for Kyper Corlox, Corlox, Corlox,   ," he yells, then waits again for the echoes to completely fade. "I know you guys are here," echoes throughout the crater. "I can help you, you, you,   ."

Chapter 64

The sky glows red as the sun sets over the canyon. Nebula and Nario walk along a scenic pathway high upon its rim.

"He showed me a picture taken from the news within the Kingdom," Nebula tells Nario. "It was him."

"You have to stay calm and collected," Nario tells her. "It wasn't him. Besides, even if it were, which it wasn't, they have nothing on us. There's no way to trace this back to us."

"What about your contacts?" Nebula asks. "What if they squeal?"

"They can't," Nario answers. "They are simply not in a position to say anything."

"He tried to access the ship. You changed the code. This looks bad," Nebula tells him.

"Which can't be shown to be anything other than coincidental," Nario replies."

"He could make it back," Nebula conjects.

"First of all, the guy in the image isn't going anywhere," Nario answers; "the entire Kingdom is after him. He's as good as gone. If they haven't captured him by now, they soon will. Secondly, that guy wasn't him."

"How can you be so certain?" Nebula asks.

"He's dead," Nario replies.

"Dead," Nebula repeats, stunned. "How do you know that?"

"My sources," Nario answers.

"He wasn't supposed to be killed," Nebula replies. "It wasn't part of the deal."

"I don't know how it happened," Nario replies; "it was an accident."

"I don't want to see you again," Nebula tells him, now with a more distant look in her eye.

"Ever?" Nario asks. "What gives?"

"I don't know," Nebula answers; "at least for now. It's better this way."

Nario stares silently into the canyon, bewildered.

Chapter 65

Vandoc sits by a fire, staring at the brilliant moons as they sharply silhouette distant trees upon the crater's rim. "Looks like I might just die in a volcano after all," he mumbles to himself as he tosses a branch onto the fire. "What the fuck, Nario," he says in a pissed-off tone; "change the code?" Then he hears the snap of a twig from within the trees just beyond the fire's range. He moves away from the light, into the darkness opposite the noise.

"Who are you?" he hears a man call out.

"My name is Vandoc," the captain answers as he steps back into the firelight.

"How do you know Kyper Corlox?" the voice asks.

"I didn't know him personally," Vandoc answers. "He's dead. Those around him have helped me to assume his identity in an attempt to help me escape."

"You're all over the news, you know," the man says angrily as he steps forth into the light. "You've put us all in a lot of danger by coming here. We're pulling out tonight because of you, asshole."

"My friends call me Vandoc," the captain replies; "and I didn't mean to put you in danger. I had nowhere else to turn."

"What do you want from us?" the stranger asks. "We can't take you with us."

"Can you just get me off Kublai?" the captain asks. "I'm in pretty deep here. I have to get off Kublai."

"No, it's too risky," the stranger answers.

"Look, you know they are closing in," Vandoc tells him. "Don't let Kyper's legacy die on this island. If not for me, do it for him. He was faithful to the end to your cause."

The stranger pauses to ponder the request, then speaks.

"I don't know that that makes any sense, morally speaking. Follow me," he tells the captain.

"Thanks," Vandoc replies. "I didn't get your name," he adds.

"And you won't," the man replies, still seemingly annoyed by the captain's presence; "but you can refer to me as General."

"The General it is," Vandoc responds.

"Just General. I gotta say, it was pretty gutsy of you to try outrunning prehistoric Siberian Unicorns," the General tells him as they walk into the night.

"Is that what that was?" Vandoc replies. "It was ignorance, not courage. I had no idea that anything like that would be on this island." General chuckles.

Vandoc is guided around the lake, across a meadow, and under a canopy of towering trees, which perfectly shield several ships. Campfires dot the local landscape.

"You brought him here?" a woman yells angrily.

"He's the guy on the news," General answers. "He needs to get off Kublai or they'll kill him," he adds before they step aside to privately quarrel over the matter. Vandoc waits patiently by. After several minutes of fighting, both General and the woman calm down.

"We now have to stop on Thorbon in the morning to stay in a shadow," General tells Vandoc; "the second moon," as he points to the sky. "It has recently been terraformed but remains mostly underdeveloped. It's largely forested and very sparsely populated. We'll leave a tent, some food, and a new, anonymous fon with you so you can follow news. Don't contact us. We'll find you if we need to. That's the best we can do for you."

"It's more than I could ever have hoped," Vandoc replies. "I'm grateful beyond words. In fact, when I get back, I'm going to find a way to help you guys, I swear."

"Back to where?" General asks.

"Mars," Vandoc answers.

"You have got to be kidding me," General replies. "You're Colonial."

"Yes," Vandoc answers; "I was abducted here on Kublai."

"You'll never gain access to the ringway, you know," General tells him.

"I don't think I need it," the captain responds. "I think I know a way around it."

"That, I'd like to see," General replies. "Look, just because we fight the Khan," he says; "don't think we are a friend of the Colonies."

"I don't," Vandoc replies; "just as someone with a common enemy."

"We leave in two hours," General tells him.

Chapter 66

"You do realize," Creed tells Boron; "how close you and I are to having our own nards fed to us on Good Morning Kingdom? One more tripped alarm, anywhere; one more any-goddamned-thing; hell, even if they catch him. We have to find and eliminate the roach, and very soon. Every cell on his scrawny body must disintegrate and go away, or you and I are going to face execution."

"The assassination plot doesn't make sense," Boron says. "I think we can assume it was coincidental."

"He couldn't have known a cargo flight would be diverted, nor board it without inside help," Creed replies. "She abetted him."

"If we go after her, she may take the matter higher up the food chain, leaving us fucked," Boron says.

"She won't," Creed responds. "She's already knee-deep in an assassination plot herself and doesn't want anyone to piece it together. I seriously doubt she wants to draw the attention to herself."

Lumina sits at her desk, scanning news updates for any word on Vandoc. Her fon alerts her to a call from Creed. She hesitates, letting it pong repeatedly. It doesn't stop. She takes it.

"How can I help you, Colonel?" she asks Creed.

"You helped him," Creed says. "You got him a new identity, and you got him on that flight. It's been you all along."

"Who and what are you talking about?" Lumina asks. "Is this about the guy you were looking for?"

"We're coming to visit you; to ask a few questions," Creed tells her in a threatening tone.

"You are always welcome here, Colonel," Lumina replies.

Meanwhile, General's ship touches down on a rolling hill on Thorbon's Seabed Plains as General shows Vandoc the ship's customized controls. Apparently, mutual trust has developed. The trees and grass sway in the breeze as the ship's ramp descends and the captain deboards. He waves gratefully to General as the ship lifts off.

Again, on his own, Vandoc finds a secluded spot to set up camp. Once situated, he takes out the fon the fleet gave him and uses it to scan the news. More pictures of himself appear from various sources, including many from within the museum. One channel is interviewing the two fishermen and showing images of Mystina Island. It seems that he managed to get off the planet in the nick of time, but what now?

He pulls out his other fon, the one from Lumina, and transfers the photo of himself with the Khan onto his new fon as back-up. He looks up at Kublai in the sky and relaxes, starting again to feel that fate is on his side. Then it hits him; he can call Lumina now with his untraced fon. He questions his judgement, but caves to his temptation and dials her work fon.

"Hello, who is this?" Lumina asks upon answering.

"It's me," Vandoc replies.

"You're alive. How did you get to Thorbon?" she asks, checking his location on her tracking equipment.

"I can't tell you over a fon, but Kyper was right," Vandoc answers. "They're real."

"Creed's coming here right now," Lumina tells him. "He knows I helped you. I don't know what to do," she adds. "I'm scared for my life."

"I never meant to put you in any danger," Vandoc says. "It's time for me to stop running. I have an idea, but I need to talk to Creed. Can you give me Creed's number?"

"Are you serious?" Lumina asks.

"Very serious. I'll tell him that I've hacked it, but I need to speak with him, "Vandoc replies.""

"He's bound to have a location tracker," she answers. "He'll know where you are."

"That's okay," Vandoc replies. "Don't worry."

Lumina sighs, then forwards the number to Vandoc.

Vandoc calls Creed.

"Who is this?" Creed immediately asks as he answers the call.

"It's me, Creed," Captain Vandoc answers; "and it is within your best interest to listen to me."

"How did you call me?" Creed asks. "What the fuck do you want?"

"You to shut your mouth, for starters," Vandoc tells him; "and don't utter my name. Boron's life depends on him not knowing I'm calling you. Send him out of the room."

"Where do you get off telling me what to …" Creed interjects before being interrupted.

"Okay, fuck off Creed. Enjoy the execution, moron,' Vandoc tells him.

"One moment," Creed tells Vandoc. "Activate the location tracker and leave," he then tells Boron. "I can see your location, Captain Piss roach," Creed says once Boron is out of the room. "How in the hell did you manage to get to Thorbon?"

"You may have noticed that I have a knack for hitching rides on passing celestial bodies," Vandoc replies.

"I've noticed that you're are an idiot," Creed responds. "You have just made my job a lot easier by escaping Kublai. What a fool for calling me on a military line. I have location tracking, you know? I'm going to find you and I'm going to kill you. You're a sitting duck."

"Maybe," Vandoc replies; "but what an odd way for you to spend your twilight hours, chasing me down," he adds with a smirk.

"You're a piss roach," Creed yells. "Whatever pant-load of roach shit you think you are dreaming up, it isn't going to work on …"

"I was there, Creed," Vandoc interrupts; "on Mythos. I slew that beast and comforted the skydeer that Boron shot, as it died. I was at the bridge on Shangdu, with the sheep, again just one step ahead of you. Now, do you think I called you out of the blue just to chat?" he asks as he transmits the picture of himself with the Khan over the fon."

"What is this?" Creed asks, looking at the picture.

"It's a selfie of the Khan and myself, which I also sent from an old Falcon transmitter in the museum, now traveling slow-beam to a relay station on Pondo via an ancient narrow band win-wave, along with a confession implementing you and Boron in a plot to assassinate the Khan," the captain tells him.""

"I have no involvement whatsoever in any plot to assassinate the Khan," Creed angrily replies.

"Save it for the judge, Creed" Vandoc says; "that is unless we beat the message to Pondo and scramble it with your ship's diffuser."

"What do you want?" Creed asks.

"Your ship, idiot, fully fueled and stocked to capacity with provisions," Vandoc replies. "I'm taking it. It's the only way I can travel undetected."

"Go fuck yourself," Creed yells. "You're lying and I'm going to kill you."

"By my calculations, Creed, our window of making Pondo is now down to minutes, not hours," Vandoc responds. "It might be a good idea for you to shut-the-fuck-up and act. Now, I thought you might reject this plan and come chase me around Thorbon, but you won't find me before they find you. That I vow. Without your help, they may catch me as well, but not before I watch your execution on Good Morning Kingdom."

"Go fuck yourself," Creed says, "you piss roach."

"Yeah, yeah, go fuck myself," Vandoc replies; "piss roach this, piss roach that. You're an asshole, Creed. Are you aware of that? Now take as much time as you like to ponder my plan. As for me, I've better things to do with my time than to listen to your sorry ass pout."

"Wait," Creed interjects; "what do I need to do?"

"Well, for starters, you need to shut that hole in your face, unless you are asked a question," Vandoc answers. "Christ, I can't stand to even look at you, let alone listen to your nonstop... Anyway, I digress. These are my conditions," he adds; "I want you to bring Magnus, my former cellmate. I don't give a damn if you make it look like he jumped into Dyvok, or what, but he's coming. I'll transmit my landing coordinates here on Thorbon. Upon touchdown, you will transfer your ship's administrative access code to me. I will board, change the code, and commandeer your vessel. At that point, yourself, your ship captain, Boron, and anyone else with you are invited to fuck-off. I will fly to Pondo, scramble the transmission, then disappear with your ship, never to be heard from again."

"You won't have ringway access," Creed says. "You can't escape the Kingdom."

"Didn't I just tell you to SHUT-THE-FUCK-UP?" Vandoc asks. "I don't need ringway access."

"I don't trust you," Creed says.

"That," Vandoc replies; "is incidental. Oh, and Creed," he adds; "you and your sorry goons are henceforth to leave Lumina completely alone. She's innocent in all of this."

Several seconds of silence ensue as Creed ponders Vandoc's plan.

"I'm going to leave Boron out of this," Creed says. "The less he knows, the better."

"I thought you might. That's why I insisted on privacy," Vandoc replies.

"How can I explain a stolen ship?" Creed asks. "Ships are only stolen in ancient tales."

"Not my issue," Vandoc tells him. "Your primary problem, I would say, is my presence in this pathetic Kingdom."

"A kidnapping would be my best cover," Creed says as he ponders the plan. "Can you leave me on Pondo?" he asks.

"If confined to the ship's guest quarters in brig mode," the captain tells him with a hint of sympathy; "but you might want to treat Magnus well," he adds. "He'll be the one attending to your needs on the flight to Pondo."

Chapter 67

Back on Pyro, Magnus sits alone in his cell. The door suddenly slides open and Creed enters. Magnus freezes in sheer fear, not even able to look Creed in the eye. What in Christ's name does he want?

Creed sits next to him on his bunk. Magnus rolls his eyes to the side of his head, but is unable to move his head, frozen in fear.

"How are you doing?" Creed asks in a mild tone. Magnus begins to shake.

"I'm fine," he answers.

"I'm glad to hear that," Creed tells him; "really."

"What do you want?" Magnus asks angrily, shaking. "Are you here to kill me? I will haunt you…"

"No, not at all," Creed says. "I want you to come with me. I'm going to take you to meet Captain Vandoc on Thorbon. He's alive and waiting for us there. You see, he and I have mended fences. Now come with me, please," Creed requests as he gets Magnus to stand with him.

"Fuck you," Magnus says. "You're not taking me to Thorbon. You're going to throw me in Dyvok. You asshole!"

"No, you've got me all wrong," Creed says. "I can see you and I got off to a bad start. Was it the pig shit? About that, I was only doing my job. I really didn't mean any harm by that. I've actually always thought that you and I have a lot in common," he continues as they walk out of the cell. Highly dubious, Magnus remains tense, still unable to even look at Creed.

The Legendary Escape of Captain Vandoc

Chapter 68

Concealed by forest, Vandoc watches from a short distance as Creed's ship stirs up a dust cloud as it touches down. Creed and his pilot emerge moments later from the vessel. The pilot sets off on foot toward a local transport station, leaving an impatient and agitated Creed beside his ship, looking around anxiously.

"Where are you, Vandoc?" he yells once his pilot is out of earshot. "Come on, time is ticking."

"That's Captain Vandoc to you," the captain says as he steps from the treeline; "and feel fortunate that I don't require you to address me as 'my wiser', but I'll let that one speak for itself. Now, we can get in front of the transmission with minutes to spare, that is once you give me administrative access to this vessel, or we can chat further. I have been dying to know how things are on Pyro."

"Let's do this, Vandoc," Creed insists.

The two approach the ship, where Creed lays his hand upon a touchpad, then cues in a series of numbers. He is prompted to confirm his decision with stern warnings. The screen asks for the new bio-data. Vandoc puts his hand on the pad. He is prompted to enter a new administrative code. He tells Creed to look away before doing so. Once confirmed, the door to the ship opens.

On board, Creed takes Vandoc to the ship's posh guest quarters, where Magnus sits nervously on the edge of his bed. He is ecstatic to see Vandoc.

"Praise Pawan," he yells in joy; "I thought you were dead." He laughs and laughs. "I thought they were planning to kill me. How the hell did you pull this off?" he asks.

"In a nutshell, I outsmarted Creed. I'll tell you all about it on the way," Vandoc answers. "Right now, we have to get to Pondo. Now, into your chambers and we'll be on our way," the captain directs Creed.

Vandoc puts the chamber in brig mode the moment Creed steps inside, making it real. The captain and Magnus look at each other smiling. They turn to Creed and begin to laugh, then even harder at his deadpan facial reaction to their laughter.

The ship lifts off, then glides over a canopy of mighty, lush green trees. Well below, Creed's ship captain stares up from the window of a speeding train, watching the ship turn upward and climb into the clouds.

Chapter 69

Back in the Ringway Café, gliding high above the Martian surface, Agent Sandbrook strokes his beard as he and Inspector Perry stare down through a viewing window, over icy craters.

"I've requested the military to deploy a mobile ringway to Cubikos in case Vandoc has discovered Notorbok. He may find a way to accelerate, but won't be able to slow down without us," Agent Sandbrook tells Inspector Perry.

"Is there any word of a capture within the Kingdom through any military channels?" Perry asks.

"No word," Sandbrook answers. "How could anyone evade such a manhunt?"

"Do you really think it was him?" Perry asks.

"Yes," Sandbrook answers; "I do."

"What does Nario have to gain?" Perry asks.

"Favor with the Kingdom," Sandbrook replies. "Perhaps a payout, or maybe he owed them. He'll get his chance in court to explain."

"And Vandoc's wife?" Perry inquires.

"She'll get hers too," Sandbrook answers.

Chapter 70

Magnus sits in the first mate's chair, next to Vandoc on the flight deck, still smiling.

"Where do you want to go?" Vandoc asks him; "I have to enter a trajectory before we break orbit."

"I have nowhere to go," Magnus answers.

"I can take you anywhere," Vandoc says. "We have our own untracked, military-brass vessel. This thing has executive privileges."

"I want to go with you," Magnus replies.

"There is a really good chance that I don't make it to where I'm going," Vandoc replies. "I'm following a hairbrained course of action that very well may be a b-line to my grave."

"Where are you going?" Magnus asks.

"I'm going to attempt to fly between the Perseus and Sagittarius arms of the Galaxy in this ship without a ringway portal," Vandoc answers.

"That's nuts," Magnus says. "Won't it take like twelve hundred years?"

"I know of an uncharted black hole, discovered inadvertently during a military reconnaissance mission during the war, below the galactic plane, not too far from the Pondo system. The pilot, who almost got pulled into it, had to redirect all his ship's resources into a controlled burn to correct his course. His book mentions the anomaly but keeps the coordinates under wraps. With my military clearance, I was able to look up his mission's flight path. If we follow the path in reverse, but steer into the vortex rather than away, we can use its gravity to slingshot across the divide."

"A black hole," Magnus says; "gee, what could go wrong?"

"We could get pulled in and pulverized for starters," Vandoc answers; "or flung in a wrong direction at a speed which we could never counter. That, or we could do everything perfectly, yet not have our distress signal received in time for us to be caught, leaving us to fly-by our target and on to our deaths."

"Sounds better than being thrown into Dyvok," Magnus says. "How long do you think it will take to cross the divide?" he asks.

"Eighteen months, plus or minus six depending how powerful the vortex is and how accurately we navigate it," Vandoc answers.

"I'm in," Magnus tells him.

"Very well," Vandoc replies; "I've set our course for Pondo. Now, shall we go check on our guest?"

Magnus and Vandoc find Creed glued to the news in the guest chambers.

"Are we going to be able to scramble the transmission in time?" Creed asks.

"Yeah, about that," Vandoc says with a grin.

"There is no transmission, is there?" Creed asks. "You lied."

"To save my life and escape a god forsaken tribe of soulless savages who illegally abducted me," Vandoc replies. "I think I can live with that one. Now, as agreed, Creed," Vandoc adds; "I will drop you off on Pondo. You were never smart enough to catch me, so face it, getting me out of the Kingdom is your next best shot at survival."

"Now, the captain and I were wondering what you would like for dinner," Magnus tells Creed.

"Really?" Creed asks.

"Really," Magnus answers.

"Come to think of it," I could go for some pepper-crusted, seared ahi tuna," Creed answers; "with some wasabi dipping sauce."

"That sounds mouth watering," Vandoc replies.

"With wasabi dipping sauce," Magnus replies, shaking his head. "Well, then it's settled," Magnus adds; "the captain and I will be having the ahi," he states.

"Can I have some?" Creed asks.

"We have prepared a special dish for you," Magnus answers; "farm-fresh pig shit, asshole. Perhaps you would like it pepper-crusted, or some wasabi dipping sauce with that?" he adds as his face breaks into laughter. Vandoc cracks up, getting more of a kick out of this new Magnus, reborn from the broken man he knew on Pyro.

Creed remains emotionless.

"Relax, Creed," Vandoc says. "We're fresh out of pig shit."

Chapter 71

At the Khan's High Command Quarters, Commander Nerabo sits at a circular conference table surrounded by the high command. A picture of Vandoc appears on the jumbo screen.

"Unbeknownst to the public, the alleged assassin has been ID'd by MIU,[7]" High Commander *Sorbo* announces as the room lights dim. "He is a military prisoner by the name of Jonathan Vandoc," he adds. "Our records show that he was assigned to and committed suicide on Pyro. Pyro," he ponders. "Under whose command is Pyro?" he asks.

"It's under my command," Nerabo answers.

"And is this the first you've learned of this?" Sorbo asks.

---

[7] **MIU**: the Khan's Military Intelligence Unit

"Yes," Nerabo answers; "but…" he reluctantly adds.

"But what?" the high commander impatiently asks.

"There have been a few reported incidents of police alarms going off that correspond with Pyro's radio-signature," Nerabo replies.

"How many and where?" the commander asks.

"Four in all," Nerabo answers; "all on Shangdu."

"And you did not report them to us?" the high commander asks.

"I contacted Colonel Creed over the matter. He told me his prisoners were all accounted for. The alarms were too erratic, indicative of malfunction," Nerabo answers.

"Bring Creed to me," the high commander instructs Nerabo. "You don't want to fail this task, trust me."

Chapter 72

Boron sits atop the throne in Creed's chamber, grinning with pride and intoxicated with the interim power bestowed upon him by Creed's absence. In front of him stands a prisoner, brought in for underperforming in the mines.

"Do you know who I am?" Boron asks the prisoner.

"Yeah," he answers; "I mean you're not Creed, but you're that other guy."

"Silence, piss roach!" Boron yells…

"Sir," a voice sounds over the room's sound system; "Commander Nerabo's ship has just landed on Creed's platform."

"What?" Boron asks as his grin drops off his face into a panic. "Why wasn't I informed of his arrival earlier?"

"It's a commander's ship, sir," the voice replies. "Such notification is not required."

The chamber doors open and in walks Nerabo with two huge, ripped guards. One is carrying a weapon and the other a briefcase.

"Where is Creed?" Nerabo asks in a raised voice.

"I don't know," Boron answers. Upon hearing this, the guard with the gun yanks him from the throne and throws him to the ground. Boron's guards and prisoner back away, then slip out of the back of the room. Boron is pinned down with his face pressed to the floor.

"He's not responding to our calls," Nerabo says. "Who would know?"

"His ship was gone when I came here," Boron says. "Try his captain. If you let me the fuck up, I can even call him for you."

Nerabo signals his goon to lift Boron up. Once standing again, he dusts himself off, pulls out his fon and dials Creed's personal captain.

"Yes, Boron," the captain answers after several seconds of delay.

"Is Creed with you?" Boron asks. Several more seconds lapse before an answer is heard.

"No," the captain replies; "he took off with the ship."

"What do you mean he took off with the ship?" Boron asks. "He can't fly."

"Yeah, I don't know," the captain answers after several more seconds of delay. "Creed told me that I could go into the village for the morning. Next thing I know, the ship is taking off."

"Where are you?" Boron asks.

"I'm on Thorbon?" the captain replies after a long delay.

"Thorbon," Nerabo yells angrily.

"At least that explains the signal delay," Boron says.

"You think?" Nerabo says. "Fuck, hook him up," he tells his goons.

The guard with the case opens it and pulls out a portable lie detector.

"God knows I hate these things," Nerabo says. "Now, I have to tell you, but I think you know, if you lie, you die." The guard attaches the device to Boron's head. "The good news is, I have only one question for you." A bead of sweat runs down Boron's temple. "Where is Colonel Creed?"

"I don't know," Boron answers, shaking. The light remains green.

"Release him," Nerabo instructs his guard as he pulls his fon out to call the high commander.

"Do you have Creed?" the high commander asks.

"No, sir," Nerabo answers; "he's gone."

"Where?" the commander asks.

"I don't know, but he abandoned his captain on Thorbon and took his ship," Nerabo answers.

"Run an overriding trace on Creed's ship," the high commander instructs his first officer. There will be an extra five years' worth of provisions awarded to any commander who brings Creed and Vandoc before me, or three years' worth for verification that they've been hunted down and destroyed."

"Yes, Sir!" the officer replies.

"As for you," the high commander tells Nerabo; "you are to return to base immediately."

"Understood, Sir" Nerabo replies with a faraway look on his face.

Chapter 73

"Let me get this straight. You kill a grasshopper on Mythos and now think you're Caribon," Magnus says in laughter as he sits with Vandoc on the flight deck, watching streaks of light move slowly across the windows.

"I just know what I know, both legend and fact. What I snuffed was no grasshopper," Vandoc replies. "It was more like a lightning fast, three-story tall mantis."

"Oh, dear prophet Caribon," Magnus jokes; "how can I serve thee?"

"You can start with a little respect," the captain answers as he tips back a bottle of wine from Creed's kitchen.

"I'd be thrilled if it were true," Magnus tells Vandoc; "if you really were Caribon."

"Really?" Vandoc asks.

"Really," Magnus answers; "because it would mean that your work is not finished.   You have yet to free my people."

"Captain," Creed's voice sounds over the video com. "There is something on the news you need to see."

"What is it, Creed?" Vandoc asks.

"We have a situation," Creed answers.

"We'll be right there," Vandoc responds.

They find Creed watching news.

"We have a ship to fly, Creed," Magnus tells him. "This had better be good."

"Do you see that man they're showing on the news?" Creed asks. "He is Commander Nerabo and he's scheduled to be executed at dawn for his dereliction of duty in connection with the plot to assassinate the Khan. They're going to broadcast it on Good Morning Kingdom."

"And what does this have to do with our current situation?" Vandoc asks.

"He is my superior; I answer directly to him," Creed responds. "This is now a military matter. They've figured it out."

"Once we make Pondo, we're as good as gone," Vandoc replies. "I don't see anything in our way on the scanners."

"You won't either," Creed replies. "A Condor-5 can't track a command ship, but they track us, and they can outrun us three-to-one."

"I thought we were untraceable," Vandoc says.

"Untraced but not untraceable," Creed answers. "Our privacy can be overridden by the high command should they deem it necessary. This is very likely our current scenario."

"They must know we're headed to Pondo," Vandoc says. "We have no choice but to stay our trajectory, but we can lose them when we slingshot around Ariq."

"If they don't intercept us first," Creed says.

"If you're right, we can't drop you on Pondo," Vandoc tells Creed.

"They're going to kill me now anyway," Creed replies; "no matter what I do."

"We are going to attempt to fly your ship out of the Kingdom. You could stay on board with us and defect to the Colonies," Vandoc suggests.

"I'd rather die," Creed replies.

"I'm cool with that," Vandoc responds with a genuine grin. "What do you think, Magnus?"

"Yeah, I'm down," Magnus answers.

"Then it's settled," Vandoc says rubbing his palms together. "We'll dump your carcass before we set out across the divide. We don't want it stinking up this ship."

Vandoc and Magnus walk away.

"Captain," Creed hollers just before they exit the room.

"What is it, Creed?" Vandoc asks.

"What would happen to me in the Colonies?" Creed asks.

"Make up your little mind," Vandoc tells him, followed by a pause and a sigh. "A military tribunal and a sentencing," he goes on to answer; "that would reflect your level of guilt in any war crimes you may have committed. They'll provide you with a lawyer and take your circumstances into consideration. Hell, if you're cooperative, you may even thrive. I will say this, and you will listen" Vandoc adds; "the worst thing that could imaginably happen to you in the UC pales in comparison to what you have put Magnus, myself, and so many others through.

"I've never considered cooperating with my enemy," Creed thinks aloud.

"People in the Colonies don't think of you as the enemy," Vandoc replies. "Nobody wants to fight the Kingdom anymore. They've moved on, developed all around your crumbling Kingdom.

Nobody is going to invade. Nobody gives a flying fuck."

"Check the hyper-com monitor," Creed tells them. "Vessel numbers that begin with a nine are command ships. If their numbers blink at all, it means they're blinding their transmissions to us. You can use the estimated transmission time, or ETT indicator to calculate how close those command ships are getting. We usually have a visual when they're transmissions are within ten seconds."

"Damn, thank you, Creed," Vandoc says slack-jawed. "Didn't think I'd ever say that," he tells Magnus.

"No, didn't see that one coming," Magnus replies.

"Let's go check the hyper-com monitor," the captain says, still shaking his head.

Chapter 74

High Commander Sorbo sits in front of a large screen monitoring his fleet's pursuit of Creed's ship. His first officer appears on screen to update him.

"Have you found him?" Sorbo asks.

"We have traced him, sir, and are in pursuit," the officer reports. "He is on a trajectory to the planet Pondo."

"Pondo?" Sorbo asks.

"A planet orbiting the blue giant Ariq, terraformed and used as a colonial base during the war. Its elliptical orbit renders it largely uninhabitable, even terraformed," the officer answers.

"Why would they go there?" Sorbo wonders out loud.

"I don't know," his officer responds; "but all roads seem to be leading to the Colonies. Do you think Creed conspired?"

"It doesn't matter now," Sorbo answers. "He obviously failed to report things. When the Khan wants a culprit, he finds one. He won't let this go without lopped heads rolling, and Creed's will be one of them."

"Incoming message from Commander Tycho," a voice announces over the sound system. A gray bearded man appears on screen, clad in a decorated military uniform.

"I'm on course to Pondo and will arrive minutes ahead of Creed and the assassin;" Tycho reports, "with Commander Shadok's vessel not far behind."

"Well done," Sorbo replies. "Maintain transmission exclusion. They have no idea we're coming. If any resistance is exhibited whatsoever, destroy Creed's vessel."

Chapter 75

On the flight deck, Vandoc and Magnus stare at the hyper-com monitor.

"I'll be damned," Vandoc tells Magnus; "the bastard is right. Look at these two. They flash more frequently and have short transmission times. They're closer, especially that one," the captain adds, pointing to the screen. "It looks like we'll have to contend with them."

"Contend with command ships!" Magnus replies with a look of fright on his face. "All of the nine numbered vessels' transmission times are decreasing. They're all coming toward us."

"They won't follow us once we break trajectory for Maladoc," Vandoc tells him. "When we steer into the vortex, we'll have to recalculate our destination; there will be no known target star to which they can redirect their course. It would be foolish to pursue us, even in a command ship, especially when they aren't prepared to navigate a black hole. They'd be wise to write us off as dead at that point and save themselves."

"This is not a good spot to be in," Magnus replies.

"Relax," Vandoc answers; "I've been in worse."

"Like," Magnus asks sarcastically; "a fight with a grasshopper? These are command ships for Christ's sake."

"Our advantage is that they don't know that we know they're coming. I have an idea," he adds with a distant look on his face. "We need Creed to go along."

Chapter 76

Commander Tycho's mighty ship reverses its outboard thrusters as it slows to enter orbit around Pondo.

"Tell the fleet we are in orbit and prepared to intercept Creed's ship," Tycho announces in a deeply serious tone.

"Sir, Creed's ship is approaching the system now," a command deck navigator announces."

"We're the only ones here," Tycho says with a proud smile. "Looks like the provisions are mine."

"They seem to be shifting trajectory, sir," the navigator announces; "now lining up with Ariq."

"Transmission to Creed," Tycho commands.

"Sending," a voice responds.

"Colonel Creed," Tycho announces; "this is Commander Tycho. You and everyone on board are to surrender at once. You cannot outrun us and you have nowhere to go." There is a moment of video noise.

"Oh, it's good to see you, Commander," Creed replies as he appears on screen. "We're having trouble with our communication system, so sorry if we cut out on you. I was taken hostage by one of my prisoners, but I have subdued him and have retaken control of my ship."

"Who's flying your vessel?" Tycho asks.

"It's been set to autopilot," Creed answers. "Otherwise, it's only me."

"Why have you shifted course for Ariq?" Tycho asks.

"The ship's course is set to whatever Captain Vandoc set it to," Creed replies. "I'm not a pilot. I can't fly this thing."

"Sir, should we just shoot them down?" Tycho's first officer asks him as the transmission is muted.

"Hold on," Tycho replies. "They can't outrun us. Let this play out," he instructs his officer. "We could use the full reward."

The Legendary Escape of Captain Vandoc

"He stole my administrative code," Creed says over the video. "I can only control the escape pods. When this ship goes into orbit, I think I can get to you via a pod."

"That doesn't make sense, Commander," Tycho's first officer tells him.

"He's an idiot," Tycho responds. "You appear to be heading to Ariq," Tycho transmits to Creed. "I'm setting a course to rendezvous with you there. Abandon ship by pod and we'll pick you and the assassin up. We'll worry about your ship later."

"He must know he has no chance of selling this story to the Khan," the first officer tells Tycho.

"He also has no motive to be involved in a plot to assassinate the Khan and run to Ariq," Tycho replies. "Relax, we've got him, one way or another. Now set course for Ariq."

Within minutes, Tycho's ship arrives at Ariq.

"We're ready to dock with your pod," Tycho announces.

"Roger that," Creed replies. "We're in orbit around Ariq, about to lose you. We'll be in two pods, ready to dock when we come around the star."

"What do you mean by two pods?" Tycho transmits angrily.

"Yes, I have the prisoner in one and the…" Creed replies as the transmission cuts out for several seconds. "So, we had to go with…" it cuts out again.

"Colonel, I'm losing you." Tycho says as the transmission goes out.

Meanwhile, on the other side of Ariq.

"Okay, we're in their shadow. Full acceleration to Maladoc," Vandoc instructs the onboard navigation system. "Prepare to release pods one and three on my count; three, two, one, and release." Two escape pods unlatch and drift closer to Ariq as Creed's ship escapes orbit.

Three-and-a-half minutes later, the pods are detected by Tycho's crew as they round the mighty sun.

"Two incoming pods," the first officer announces.

"Shields down and prepare to dock," Tycho instructs. "Where's the ship?" he asks.

"It has yet to come into view," his navigator answers.

"We're on approach," Creed is heard saying. "Requesting docking."

"Creed, we lost communication," Tycho says. "Why two pods?"

The Legendary Escape of Captain Vandoc

"Preparing to dock," Creed announces, not answering Tycho as the pods come into clear view.

"We had to use two pods to..." Creed says just before cutting transmission.

"Decelerate and prepare to dock," Tycho transmits as the approaching pods drift closer. There are no lights luminating on either pod and neither seems to be slowing. "Evasive action," Tycho yells as the speed of the pods increases. "Shields up and fire on those pods!"

Cannons fire at the pods from the mammoth ship, but the pods shift direction just as they near it, each now steering toward a separate main thruster. One pod is struck by anti-spacecraft fire and explodes just before striking its targeted thruster. The other is a direct hit on the ship's other main thruster. Both pods succeed in carrying out their missions nonetheless. Two brilliant explosions light the deep dark sky, both brief, extinguished by the vacuum of space. Axillary lights illuminate where large portions of the ship's lighting system fail as it drifts aimlessly above Ariq.

"Sir, it appears Creed's ship has escaped orbit at a high velocity," Tycho's navigator says.

"You don't say?" Tycho replies, shaking his head.

Chapter 77

"High Commander Sorbo," an automated voice says over the Khan's High Command Quarters; "Colonel Creed's vessel is on a trajectory to Maladoc."

"Direct all command ships to Maladoc," Sorbo announces.

From his hobbled ship's viewing deck, Commander Tycho watches a glaring dot through a sun-shielded window slingshot around Ariq.

"Go get those piss roaches, Commander Shadok," Tycho transmits. "Do not trust Creed. He's in on it. Blow them out of the sky."

"This is Commander Shadok," a voice announces over the comm; "rounding Ariq on course for Maladoc. The target has disappeared into the clouds of the nebula Canis Major. Last ping has them on trajectory for Maladoc. Will keep you informed."

A mere quarter light-year in front of them, Vandoc and Magnus stare again at the hyper-com monitor.

"That ship is closing in fast," Magnus says as he watches its transmission time wind down like a bomb. "I think we're fucked."

"Not yet," Vandoc says, running across the deck to look at the heading indicator. "Prepare to shift course in ten seconds," he tells them as he watches their heading. The ship's outboard engines fire. On the ten-second mark, the ship alters heading.

"Why did we change course?" Magnus asks.

"We're mirroring Commodore Trebok's flight in reverse. We should be entering the area where he was pulled off course within seven minutes."

"Who?" Magnus asks.

"Never mind," Vandoc answers. "Where are you, Notorbok?"

"We'll be within range of the command ship's cannons within seconds," Magnus warns.

"Hold on," Vandoc says. "Wait for it."

"Wait for what?" Magnus asks in a panic.

An alarm sounds. Vandoc smiles as they listen.

"Ship veering off trajectory," an onboard voice announces. "Course correction required."

"Wait for that," Vandoc yells as he scrambles to the console. "From what direction is the source of the intervening force?" he asks the onboard navigator as he types frantically into the keyboard. "Yes, there, change heading to altitude 34.593 and azimuth to negative 114.909"

"Off trajectory," the onboard voice announces. "Warning, velocity increasing."

"Transmission time between us is increasing," Magnus cheerfully reports.

Shadok stands on the command deck of his ship.

"They've emerged from the Canis Major Nebula," his navigator reports, "but they've changed course."

"Changed course?" Commander Shadok asks. "Where could they possibly be going?"

"Nowhere, sir," the navigator answers. "There's nothing out there. It's foolish of them, especially in that ship. There's no celestial body to sling them back."

"Pursue them," Shadok commands.

"It's risky," his navigator says; "and we have no way of knowing their precise trajectory without a destination."

"Pursue them," Shadok restates.

Lights continue to blink on the console as Captain Vandoc keeps working the dials, honing in on Notorbok.

"Damnit, I keep overcorrecting," he yells as he tries to steer the vessel toward the black hole.

The Legendary Escape of Captain Vandoc

"You are within the margin of error," the onboard voice announces as a light turns green.

"Yes," Vandoc yells. "Full throttle ahead," he commands the ship. "I've got it!"

The thrusters ignite, sinking Magnus and Vandoc deep into the foam of their seats. Creed flies into a wall in his quarters. The ship accelerates with everything it has.

"You're going to burn up all the fuel," Creed says over the comm. "We'll have no chance of returning."

"That's the point," Vandoc replies; "the faster we rush headlong into this hole, the faster we get across the divide. We're not going back."

"I hope you know what you're doing," Creed says, just as an explosion is heard, rattling the ship."

"Warning, veering off trajectory," the onboard voice warns after the explosion.

"Damnit," Vandoc yells as he rapidly enters data into the computer, trying to correct the ship's course; "we can't take another hit like that. Shields on full," he commands the ship's computer. "Execute a rifle roll." The ship begins to rotate around its axis.

"What's going on?" Magnus asks.

"It makes us a much harder target," Vandoc answers.

"Course corrected," the onboard voice reports.

Commander Shadok stares intensely at his monitor as he emerges from the Canis Nebula.

"We have them in range," his navigator reports. "Their shields are up and they've taken evasive action. Our cannons may have damaged them."

"Keep firing," Shadok instructs.

"Something's wrong, sir," the ship's first officer reports.

"What now?" Shadok asks, frustrated.

"Their velocity has increased well beyond their ship's capabilities," the officer reports; "as has ours. We're being pulled by an unknown source and may not be able to reverse our course if we continue."

"Pursue," the commander yells.

"Commander, incoming transmission from Creed's ship," Shadok's communication officer announces.

"Onscreen," Shadok commands. Captain Vandoc appears.

"So, the assassin is steering the ship," Shadok says.

"Look, Commander; Vandoc replies; "I'm no assassin. That, however, is neither here nor there. You have a bigger issue at hand. In case you haven't noticed, your velocity is increasing. That's because you are flying headlong into a black hole. If you reverse thrust with everything you've got right now, you may yet climb back out of here. Otherwise, I hope you have prepared yourself to navigate a black hole."

"Fire everything we've got at them," Shadok yells.

Creed's ship is struck several times, but the shields and Vandoc's rifling maneuver manage to keep it on course. Then it appears before them in the distance; Notorbok. Their ship's velocity continues to increase.

Soon thereafter, Notorbok's event horizon silhouette through thick hydrogen clouds comes into view of Commander Shadok's crew.

"Commence retro-thrust," Shadok immediately commands as he stares at light flowing over the edge, disappearing into the mighty void.

"Commencing retro-thrust," his first officer echoes. The ship begins to slow.

"Sir, deceleration rate is falling off," his navigator reports. "We may not be able to reverse course."

"Full retro thrust," Shadok yells.

"Sir, if that fails, we'll slow to nothing, only to be pulled into that hole," his navigator warns.

"Full retro," Shadok commands; "we're getting out of here."

"Full retro thrusters," his first officer responds.

Shadok's ship slows as it tries to move in the opposite direction of Notorbok's pull. Creed's ship fades out of sight as it races toward the massive void. Shadok now knows his only hope is to fly toward the vortex in order to increase speed, use the hole's gravity to slingshot, then time a burn to escape its orbit.

"Full thrust along target ship's last known trajectory," Shadok commands.

Vandoc and Magnus stare at the event horizon, watching it suck light into sheer blackness.

"Our hyperlight velocity will swing us beneath the event horizon," Vandoc tells Magnus; "technically inside the hole. Centrifugal force will increase gradually, then let up should we survive." Colorful hydrogen clouds thicken as their ship nears Notorbok. "Holy hell, look at how fast we're going," Vandoc points out to Magnus.

"Escape velocity estimated," the onboard system announces as the ship glides over the black hole's horizon.

"Praise Pawan," Vandoc yells. "Plot and initiate maximum velocity course to the planet Cubikos upon first escape window," he instructs the onboard system.

"Initiated," the system responds. "Escape burn ignition in three minutes and thirty-one seconds on mark," followed by a beep.

The ship flows into the event horizon like a raft on a river of light.

"Strap into your seat," Vandoc tells Creed over the comm system; "we're going in." Magnus and Vandoc are pulled deeply downward, into their gyroscopic command chairs as the ship reaches the black hole's point of perigee, swinging ever-so-near the vortex. Like sinking into an ocean of emptiness, their vessel sinks below the flow of lights, deeper into the hole. Aside from a glow, the only light they can now see is from the crest of the event horizon, which now flows well above them in bending beams of light. At hyperlight speeds well beyond those ever reached by Creed's ship, the three men sit in silence. The sensation they feel is dream-like, very surreal. Their fears fade into pure bliss as they glide beneath a ceiling of light in an uncharted dome of darkness.

"Commencing escape burn," the system announces. The ship rattles as the outboard engines fire once again, redirecting the ship's course. The rattle turns into a violent shake as the ship climbs back out of the void, into the clouds of swirling hydrogen and bending light. Vandoc, Magnus, and Creed all hang on with all they've got to their chairs' armrests as the shaking ship creaks under immense pressure.

"The ship's breaking up," Magnus says. "It's not gonna hold."

"Press the transmit button," Vandoc tells Magnus as they hang on with all they've got.

"Why?" Magnus says as he presses the button.

"It's an attempt to transmit our first distress signal," Vandoc tells Magnus.

"What good is that going to do us?" Magnus asks as he presses the button.

"For our immediate situation, none," Vandoc answers; "but if that transmission manages to make it out of here and we don't, at least history will know we got this far."

Chapter 78

The velocity indicator on Shadok's Ship slows, then speeds up, then slows again, in an ongoing cycle as the ship sinks below the event horizon. A large moan is heard as its structural integrity gets put to the test under immense gravitational pressure.

"Plot course based on first available escape window," Shadok commands the onboard navigational system, now looking for any way out.

"No window can be found," the system replies; "escape velocity is unattainable."

"How about an orbital velocity?" Shadok asks.

"Also unattainable," the system replies; "only a decaying orbit."

"Optimise our decay for longest possible time and send a distress signal," Shadok commands. "Seek alternative course," Shadok commands his navigator.

"I have another course of action in mind if I may," the navigator replies.

"What is it?" Shadok asks.

"I thought I'd do whatever I want and you could bite my ass," the navigator tells him. "I have watched you fuck up time and again, ignoring the advice of people way smarter than yourself, such as myself, as you have pursued mistake after fu-cking mistake. Now you have done it. You heard her; there is no escape nor orbital velocity attainable. We're about to be obliterated and scattered hundreds of millions of light years in opposite directions thanks to your petty, narcissistic ego, and you want to send a distress signal. Have me shot if you will. We're dead anyway. I'm going to the arboretum to die in peace," he says as he walks toward the flight deck exit.

"Shoot him," Shadok instructs a sentry at the deck entrance. The guard pulls his weapon out but can't bring himself to aim it at the navigator. "Then I'll shoot him," Shadok yells as he pulls the gun from the guard's hand. Seeing this, the navigator sends the weapon flying across the room with a swift kick. Weaponless, Shadok charges, wrestling the navigator to the ground. The two exchange punches before the navigator delivers a wind-knocking upper cut, forcing the commander to drop to his knees.

"This worm isn't even worth it," the navigator says as he leaves the flight deck. The other crew members follow him out, leaving the commander on his knees, bleeding from his mouth as he tries to catch his breath.

Once inside the arboretum, the crew members activate the ship's entertainment system. A simulated sun, so convincingly real, rises behind tropical vegetation. Clouds fill the sky. Everyone gathers around a large central waterfall, staring blankly at its endless flow as the ship begins to vibrate violently. The serene sound of flowing water fades into creaking noises as the ship buckles under tremendous pressure.

On the flight deck, Shadok climbs into the captain's chair, staring at the flashing beams of light that surround the shaking ship. The vibrations intensify, leaving only a ringing in his ear.

"HEEEEYYYY," his voice can be heard screaming as his ship explodes into a debris field.

Creed's ship stops vibrating as it levels off. Vandoc, Magnus, and Creed sit unconscious, secured in their chairs, all having blacked out from G-forces reached during their escape burn. Creed is the first of them to awaken.

"Where are we, guys?" Creed asks over the comm. "Are you guys alive? Hello? Hello?" he continues, waking Vandoc.

"I'm here," Vandoc replies.

"What happened?" Creed asks. "Where are we?"

"Let me see," Vandoc replies as Magnus awakens.

"Where are we?" Magnus asks.

"On course to Cubikos!" Vandoc says laughing. "Holy hell, look at our velocity. I'm transmitting a new distress signal now. Hopefully someone gets it ahead of our arrival, which looks to be in, let's see," as he enters numbers into a keyboard; "nineteen months." The excitement fades from Magnus' face.

"Oh well," Creed says over the comm, still listening in; "I'm in no rush."

"Creed, if your ship isn't sufficiently supplied for the journey, protocol is that we eat you," Magnus tells him.

"We may not have ahi every night," Creed replies; "but we're amply stocked."

"On a serious note, Creed" Vandoc says; "your information likely saved our skin."

"Old colonel tricks, Captain," Creed replies; "kept up our sleeves in the event that we find ourselves on the run, as it appears I have."

"Well, thank you," Vandoc tells him. "I still think you are an asshole, but you've shown us another side. I will ensure that your actions are reported to proper authorities when or if we reach colonial shores."

"Thank you, Captain," Creed replies. "May you make it home."

"If I have a home," Vandoc replies.

"What makes you say that?" Magnus asks.

"Home is an illusion. I've been gone for some time," Vandoc answers. "Hell, I still don't even know how I ended up in the Kingdom, but someone close to home sold me out," he adds.

"Someone who knew of your military expertise I'd guess," Creed suggests.

"How would you know this?" Vandoc asks.

"Maxiums Krylok," Creed answers.

"Who is Krylok?" Vandoc asks.

"There is no Max Krylok," Creed responds. "Krylok is an old word for reward, or bounty. When a prisoner mentions Max Krylok, it's code from his bounty hunter, or abductor in your case, to have received maximum bounty for his involuntary service. It tells us you have skills that we need to exploit."

"So, that's why I was promoted," Vandoc says.

"It also kept you protected," Creed tells him. "Nobody will ever ask a Max Krylok about his military history, especially not under oath. If you served in the war, by law, you'd be executed and they don't want that. They want to exploit your skills. So, you're far less disposable to the Khan than others."

A red light blinks on the command console, then fades.

"What was that?" Magnus asks.

"A distress signal," Vandoc answers.

"They didn't make it out, did they?" Magnus asks, referring to Commander Shadok and crew.

"No, they didn't make it out," Vandoc answers.

Chapter 79

Four months and three weeks later, Agent Sandbrook sits at his desk at the Martian Office of Military Intelligence, laughing as he watches a sitcom while eating his lunch.

"Sir," a voice comes over the office sound system.

"What is it?" Sandbrook asks. "It's my lunch break."

"You asked me to inform you the moment anything was detected from Cubikos," the voice replies.

"Cubikos?" Sandbrook asks. "What have you got?"

"A distress signal from a hyperlight object traversing the divide. It's point of origin is unknown, but estimated to be closer to the Perseus Arm, below the galactic plane, on course for Cubikos."

"It's him," Sandbrook says. "Send a high request for permission to deploy the mobile ringway. They've been wanting to test it. This is what it was designed for."

"Request sent," the voice replies.

"Prepare my shuttle," Sandbrook orders. "Let's go get him!"

Chapter 80

Three days and five months beyond Notorbok, the captain, Magnus, and Creed continue to race through an endless night.

"We're going to die out here," Creed yells.

"Will you shut up, please!" Magnus implores. "If that's so, your constant whining isn't helping a damn thing."

"We're not even a third of the way there," Creed tells him. "There's nothing around us but complete darkness. I don't even see stars anymore."

"We have everything we need," Vandoc tells them.

"What if they don't receive our distress call in time?" Creed asks.

"Then they'll see us when we fly by Cubikos and take necessary measures to secure our arrival."

"That sounds pretty wishful," Creed replies.

"Look, if it weren't for me," Vandoc tells him; "you'd be dangling from a rope on Good Morning Kingdom."

"At least I'd be out of my misery," Creed responds.

"Warning," the onboard voice announces; "object has moved into our path. Adjust course immediately to avoid impact."

"What could be out here?" Creed yells.

"Wait," Vandoc says as he runs to the flight deck. "Identify object," he instructs the onboard scanner.

"There are a series of circular objects perfectly aligning in our flight path," the system responds.

"It's them," Vandoc yells. "They got the distress signal."

Moments later, the first ring comes into view. Creed's ship rifles straight through it, slowing down progressively while passing through. The second ring then appears, perfectly aligned. The ship passes through it, again slowing significantly. The third ring brings the ship to a floating standstill. A colonial military ship then docks. Agent Sandbrook boards through a hatch with a military guard and a doctor by his side.

"Captain Vandoc," Sandbrook says; "welcome home."

"Who are you?" Vandoc asks.

"I'm Agent Sandbrook with Colonial Forces," Sandbrook answers. "I'm here to take you home."

Vandoc stands in shock. His eyes moisten as his face relaxes.

"We're a long way from Cubikos," Vandoc tells him. "How did you get here?"

"You're the first to use our newest technology," Sandbrook answers; "mobile ringways, but please do not repeat anything you see. The technology is proprietary. Now, who is with you?" he asks.

"This is Magnus, a Pawani who would like to defect from the Kingdom," Vandoc answers; "and this is Colonel Creed, who would also like to defect."

"Please come aboard, gentlemen," Sandbrook tells them. "We'll get you checked out with our physician and processed. As soon as we get the rings realigned with Mars, we'll be on our way home."

Chapter 81

Vandoc enters his condo, where he finds Nebula on the balcony, looking out over the canyon with a glass of wine in her hand.

"Hi Neb," Vandoc says, stepping onto the deck.

"Oh my god, you're alive!" she replies. Staring intensely into his eyes, she approaches him and puts her arms around him. "I thought you were dead. Oh my god, I missed you so, so much."

"There were moments when I really missed you too," Vandoc tells her; "deeply."

"Really?" Nebula replies.

"Nario was taken into custody minutes ago," Vandoc tells her; "in connection with my abduction into the Kingdom."

"Oh my god," Neb responds; "I've always been a little suspicious of Nario..."

"SAVE IT for the judge, Neb," Vandoc tells her. "He has recordings of you. He knew you'd try to throw him under the bus. It's over. Agent Sandbrook is standing right outside this door, waiting to take you into custody."

Nebula stands stunned for a few seconds, then relaxes as her reality sinks in.

"I never wanted to hurt you," she tells Vandoc as tears roll down her cheeks.

"I hope you find help, Neb. I really do," Vandoc tells her.

"You may not believe this," Nebula tells him; "but I've never been more deeply in love with you than I am at this moment."

"I believe you," Vandoc replies; "but that, is incidental."

Agent Sandbrook, Inspector Perry, an officer and Magnus enter the condo. They take Nebula into custody, leaving Magnus and Vandoc alone in the condo.

"A lot nicer than our cell on Pyro," Magnus says as he looks around the place.

"You can have the downstairs den," Vandoc tells him. It's private, cozy, and has its own washroom. You're welcome to stay here as long as it takes you to find your own way, my friend."

"Thanks," Magnus says with a quick bow of gratitude.

Captain Vandoc pours himself a fat glass of Pinot and perches on his balcony, overlooking the canyon. As he thumbs through news articles on floating screens, he hears the Canyon Express in the distance. He pauses in a moment of pure bliss as the sound fades into a news broadcast.

"Iridium contracts soared to new heights after trade talks with the Kingdom seem to have stalled completely. In other news, Martian real estate has risen sharply for the seventeenth straight month after carbon issues with Martian carbon regulation were resolved, bringing the Martian climate back to sustainable levels…"

Vandoc logs-in to his Martian Markets trade account.

"Jesus, I really have been away," he says laughing, looking over his windfall.

Chapter 82

Inside the Caribon Café, Vandoc and Magnus sit at a bistro table, laughing as they look at all the Pawani symbols painted on the walls. Beneath a corner spotlight stands a podium with the Book of Time perched on it, open to a page mid-book titled Foreboding of the Porlock. There's a drawing on the page of a mighty, hairy beast attacking an ancient village.

"To think," Vandoc says; "that book has sat here, most likely open to that same page, since before I went to Kublai."

"So?" Magnus asks.

"So?" Vandoc responds astonished. "It remains open to a story foretelling my slaying of that beast."

"So, you really think you killed that thing," Magnus asks, pointing to the beast.

"It looked nothing like that," Vandoc says.

"Oh, that's right, it was a locust," Magnus replies chuckling.

"A mantis, more like," Vandoc says. "The picture is wrong."

"You mean the picture in the book is wrong?" Magnus asks; "not the one in your head?"

"So how were your dinners?" their server asks with a smile.

"The pioneer pies were scrumptious," Magnus replies; "very authentic," he adds; "but the Pawani dipping sauce didn't taste that authentic to me."

"Oh," Vandoc says laughing; "so, the dipping sauce is a little less than authentic, but the Porlock is accurate?" he questions.

The two shake their heads in laughter as they raise their glasses in a toast, riding high on their new freedom. Phobos sits in the Martian sky, just above the canyon rim, so close you can almost touch it. They stare silently at it, basking in the moment.

To the reader, thank you…

www.ingramcontent.com/pod-product-compliance
Lightning Source LLC
Chambersburg PA
CBHW060854250626
47159CB00008B/2730